TRAIN

In January of 2003, a Muslim fundamentalist group calling itself "Dragons for Jihad" firebombed Ethiopian publisher Russom Damba's printing press in Rabat, Morocco. They firebombed him for publishing this very book you are holding in your hand. Out of fear for his life and his family's life...he announced to the world that he was dropping Kola Boof from his publishing company.

Although more than 100 newspapers around the globe reported the firebombing of Kola Boof's publisher...only one (*The New York Post*)...reported the story in the United States, and although the Sudanese born black woman writer is an American citizen...there was virtually no concern for her situation from either the American writer's community or from American media, including black media outlets such as Essence magazine, Black Issues Book Review and BET.

"Long Train to the Redeeming Sin", which was the #1 bestselling book of 2002 at the African American Literary Book Club (www.aalbc.com), was forced out of print for the entire year of 2003.

Several months later, on April 9th 2003, an investigate human rights body (Freedom House of New York) found definitive evidence that an *illegal* fatwa death sentence had been issued against Kola Boof by members of the Government of Sudan and presented a report concerning the death threats on the floor of the United Nations in Geneva, Switzerland. None of these facts, however, helped Miss Boof to find an American publisher willing to put her work back in print.

I, an African American businessman, am proud to put this book back in print and to reissue it for Women's History Month, 2004.

Although she is a controversial, provocative author...I wish Kola Boof all the best in her struggle to present her art uncensored. Check soon for her powerful first novel, *"Flesh and the Devil"*.

Cornel Chesney
Publisher

Kola Boof's

"Long Train to the Redeeming Sin"

(Stories about African Women)

---

*Originally published by

Russom Damba in Europe and North Africa

as

"The Goddess Flower: Stories by Kola Boof"

(1998)

Door of Kush Publications

Also available in America by KOLA BOOF:

Nile River Woman

Flesh and the Devil

Politically Inspired (Anthology by Stephen Elliott)

+ This book is printed in the United States of America.
Copyright (2004) KOLA BOOF

Door of Kush Publications

Snail Mail: P.O. Box 41 Burbank, Ca. 91503
Email: doorofkush@yahoo.com
Fax Number: 909-595-5868
Book Design by Marilyn Morse, Graphics 2

ISBN: 0-9712019-0-0

***Back cover photo of Kola Boof "pregnant"
was photographed by Kangman (Quentin).**

I hearby dedicate this book to the
most prolific and important Black filmmaker
of this century and the previous one,
Mr. Ousmane Sembene of Senegal.
May God recommend him to us.

and to my new hero...Shoshana Johnson
God bless and uplift you, sister.
I love you.

Ajowa Ifetayo of Washington, D.C.,
I owe you my life! Thank you sister for drawing
attention to the dire situation of me and my babies.
It was you who forced the media to tell our story.

KOLA'S INTRODUCTION:

"The Kiss of God's Wife" is the indigeonous name that ancient Nile River nilotic peoples gave to Africa...actually meaning all the black people and their tribes counted as one. Our land, its people and the Sun: *The Kiss of God's Wife.* The outside world, however, called our land "Aithiop" or "Ethiopia"--Ethiopia originally meaning, as it means in the Christian Holy Bible...the entire continent of Africa. Cush (Sudan), Nubia (Sudan), Kenyaku, Congot, Punt (Somalia), Axum Empire (now called Ethiopia, the country) and Kamit (Egypt) were all once part of the *continent* of Ethiopia. Or Africa, or...the Kiss of God's Wife.

tima usrah.

I am a Sudanese-American writer. I am Animist-Secular, born Sunni. I consider myself, without *compromise or apology*, an African woman artist independent of any political or religious group affiliation. I am against slavery in Sudan. As a womanist, I oppose all Islamic governments, especially the evil Arab rulers of my homeland, Sudan.

Because I have been protected most of my life in the United States and feel an inexplicable bond of love towards the Black Americans--it hurts me very deeply that I have never been able to relate to them or be family with them. There is a message that I have always known it was important to share with them, but *how* to do that--it's very frustrating. So I wrote these short stories. My personal message to the Black Americans. If they read *each* one very carefully, then they will gain enpowerment and be blessed--as *I* intended for them; in an authentic way.

acknowledgements (2004):

I have to thank **Troy Johnson** for using his web site to put me on the map in the United States. He agrees with little of what I say or do, yet he supports my right to exist. His web site (**www.aalbc.com**) is a blessing to our community. I adore him.

I thank **Professor Derrick Bell** for being not only a surrogate father to me...but to many young, anonymous women who have the legacy of his activism in academia and in literature with which to know that heroic black men who care about black women do, miraculously, still exist. Derrick Bell is my hero and one of my favorite people of all time. He is nothing less than PERFECT.

My best friend **Alicia Banks** (I love you, Queen!) and my sisters **Ajowa Ifetayo, Egybira High-Ameyaw, Carole Chehade, Trula Breckenridge,** and **Gaylon Roberson**. These are my goddess flowers.

I thank **Cornel Chesney** for locating investors to put my work back into print. I love him. I thank **KJLH radio** for bringing me to Cornel. I also send a big hug to my twin sister **Linda Watkins** (author of "Althea"), author **Tracy Price Thompson** for being so kind, hello to **Kendra Williams** in Michigan, author **Chris Hayden** in St. Louis!, to my beloved **Keith Boykin** for his clarity and "bits" of advice. Keith has one of my favorite web sites (**www.keithboykin.com**). *Charles Brister (Mr. UniteUs), Joe Madison** and **Ian McGarry**, I love you all. **Yukio**, I miss your calculating intelligence, sister. **Daniecia** and my girls at **Howard University**, bless you! **ABM**, I love you and I apologize, King. Hello to **SisGal, Carey and Soul Sista**...**Tee Royal**, thanks for blessing our whole industry. You're the gatekeeper.

I thank my readers...for understanding my pain and my determination to say things that nobody wants to hear...but things that must be said. In order to let them go.

Stories

<u>Always Remember:</u>

"The world did not begin...on the
day that *you*
were born."

--Auntie Ramah (Sudan)

the lioness

O nce upon a time...and this is true...there lived in the ancient Cushite Empire, a very wealthy architect who dabbled in ivory tusk trading and was called Kueth. Very handsome and charismatic was Kueth, and because it was our law, Kueth, the original mama-tit boy, became both stool and master over some of the most treacherous yet infinitely vulnerable women in all the Nile River--Cushite Valley.

In fact, one of Kueth's seven wives, the one he paid the least attention to but the one his children liked best was a devoted loving woman called Etah. She had big feet like a camel's, was the color of slippery black jet-dark ebony and made up for being taller than every man in the clan by giving birth to seven sons and outworking, outcooking, everybody's wife, mother, sister, daughter and slave until the day she died. But unfortunately, the *evil eye* fell upon her.

Etah's watcher was Soti, a jealous co-wife. It didn't matter that young and beautiful-looking Soti was Kueth's favorite wife. BANA (you remember): *"Soti"* couldn't even keep milk on her stomach because of the way our village griots beheld Etah.

It was our tribe's animist wise men, in fact. The ones

who could actually hold conversations with the sun, who had stood over Etah before everyone in the village...their protruding bellies white with ash and their long, wormlike penis's exposed and decorated palm green...officially forgiving Etah her *tallness*. It was forgiven, they said, because she had faithfully and sincerely shown to every man's foot how truly she cherished the experience of being a good and decent; an obedient wife.

Soti, the sexy leopard, had watched on with great envy.

"Kiss Etah's feet", the Gods commanded the other women. And so Etah's feet were kissed by hundreds that day. No more would her great height be considered inferior or un-attractive, and as well, with the birth of the sixth male, then the seventh phallus--Etah received the status of manhood herself. She became one of only nine women who were allowed to eat with the men and inhale blue smoke from the hole in the WoldeAmun stone. Maleness, because each of these women had given birth to exceed six boychilds each.

Etah had never expected such glory for herself! So she stood very humbly that day, accepting the spear Kueth handed her, weeping in *irhala*. Our mothers kissing her feet sweetly.

Even Soti, the glamorous co-wife from Kamit (Egypt's real name) was behaving like a daughter born of that clan, yet the valley between Soti's thighs was covered with the inky-black fur of a menstrating tarantula, and her eyes kept darting back and forth above big white teeth and a pointed nose. Hers was that tribe of Mediterranean Sea Africans...who used to eat their newborn's afterbirth. *Kasha!*

~~

Soti had kissed the large charcoal feet that day and had made irhala (*verbal sounds that represent a smile*) to the tall, regal Etah--but not without licking off some of the crust that covered the top of Etah's foot. Certainly, Soti intended to cast a curse from the dead skin...and held it on her tongue very carefully. Awaiting nightfall.

Her fingers unwrapped the camel's hair from the belly-button of Etah's seventh infant that night. Her dark hoonta bon bon eyes (the happy chocolates) flickered behind now famous Kamitian eye makeup--black kohl sickles pointing at the ears. Soti's pink tongue danced up like a cobra to the tip of her nose and one finger touched the dead foot skin to the blood of her saved monthlies. Then dried delicately.

Carefully, she sang:

Eet--ama hajii...n'kun...jinn

Eet--ama hajii...n'kun...jinn

"A cobra will slither out of Kamit. And bring with her the carefully poisoned afterbirth of a Hebrew slave fetus. For Etah. Issi tojo, Etah!" Beautiful-looking Soti awaited the death snake.

~~

Etah took Kueth his meal the next morning, just before the cold northern winds gave way to a sunrise of instant tropical heat. She sat down a bowl of cool water, some smoked white ants rolled in spiced goat's skin, sudd-greens and whole grain stewed with honey and whatever dates the village Chief had spared for males of peer. Etah bowed her head as Kueth raised his naked body from the slick of mudd he bathed in and urinated quickly in the vase she presented. A younger wife, the one he'd poked all night, was out sweeping his Otuho stones already...and Kueth chuckled at the sound of his many children calling so early for Etah to come and play with them. But a man comes first--even before infants!

"The children", laughed Kueth, "cannot wait to see you wiggle your bottom this morning, dear wife. You had better practice new tricks to top the old ones, yes? Amuse me, dear wife."

Etah made irhala (verbal smiles) and, as Kueth began to eat his meal, she twirled around so that her firm, muscular buttocks was in full view...and then began to move her butt muscles so that the deep ritual scars of her flesh turned into themost incredibly life-like faces! Kueth laughed a thousand laughs and gave her a good, affectionate slap on the ass. He said, "You must teach the prettier women to do this, yes?"

"For the master of my heart...anything."

"Good. Then don't forget Soti's daughter today. It is time for her to be properly cut, yes? I am counting on her purity and beauty to fetch a king-sized dowry someday. For much time now--the girls only trust you to do the cutting. They say you cause the less pain and no one has died at your hands."

11

"Only because I've had no witches, kind husband. A witch shows herself by dying from the purification."

"Good", nodded Kueth as he ate the delicious meal. "Then take Soti's daughter out on the Nile today and make her pure. In addition to this idea, let me decree another: *I want Soti purified as well.* Being the Kamitian daughter of a tax collector, she has not been properly cut. They don't do it in Kamit quite the way we do. Tell her that it is my order that she be cut today with our daughter. It doesn't honor ones foot that his favorite wife be impure."

"Yes, kind husband", replied Etah as she backed out of his morning-time quarters--delighting in his respect for her. She could not wait to express her love for Soti and Tifa by cutting them.

One of the village slaves, his chest nearly hidden by the large plate in his mouth that stretched his bottom lip nearly to his navel, dutifully beat on his drum a summons for Soti to arrive at the women's granary and to bring little Tifa with her.

Etah sharpened her best blades...awaiting no snakes.

~~

"We will go to a place that I know of", Etah told Soti in that soothing goddessa voice of traditional black women.

Soti only stared at Etah's coal black face. Stricken and terrified from memories of the Kamitian version of this excruciatingly painful ritual that had already been performed on her--only in Kamit, they didn't remove the worm from the woman's flower--they simply cut the father's name in one lip and the name of the village high priest in the other. Later, if the groom requested, his title would be added. But Etah was going to remove the *worm*...tribal belief in these parts being that...if not cut, the female worm grew very long, like a man's snake, and then the woman was impure and developed mannish desires and dreamt of male privileages.

Soti wept and began the sojourn with Etah, little Tifa holding her hand but submerged in a well of silent fear. There was no sisterly chat between the two black women, because no rich man's wife, thought Soti, should be so pathetic as Etah.

For in Etah's *darkness*, Soti was reminded of the stories of the world being made, and for that impeachable blackness and for the crime of bringing the world into being--Soti hated Etah's coloring. On a man, it was understood. But on a woman...it was a reminder of women's bleeding and the beginning of that bleeding...and the guilt and very meaning of womanhood. The Kamitians (Egyptians) had a saying: "The blacker she is...the more woman she is. Too much woman blocks the sun." This is very important to understand.

For when..."*rain was new*", all humans knew that the world began from the Red Dragon--charcoal black Asli Nalla, the first human being, menstrated (the red dragon) on a rock and thus ended the Edenic period that many Africans call "the time before time began". The original earthling tribe, who actually lived in the African garden, who were from another

13

planet and could fly and whose age was in the hundreds, along with the great dinosaurs, they all perished because of Alisi-Nalla's bet with the Creator that she would survive just as well in the garden without her magic powers, and so...left alone, Alisi-Nalla was made to bleed and *feel*. It didn't help that PhumKut (the white worm of everlasting evil--part of all blood now) slithered afoot and impregnated her.

Only Asli-Nalla and her species (human beings) survived the beginning of her bleeding. Later, the Kamitian Rah adopted these facts but changed them so that a male, Alisi-Nalla's firstborn, her husband, King Nall: *"Ejaculated the universe into being."* Therefore, the Kamitian (Egyptian) versions of this story are recorded on their wall etchings, but they lie!--the much older Cushitic version is the true, accurate story of human creation. Not the Hebrew myth of Adam and Eve (who were born much, much later), not the Egyptian myth, not the Islamic stories--but our Ethiopic-Cushiphone folkway is the *naked* fact. Queen Asli-Nalla was the beginning of mankind's sojourn.

And so you understand a thing now. Because of Etah exsisting, because of her blackness, thought Soti, *every* woman suffered eternally. And even today, many Africans hold this against the original Ethiopian, because they want to return to our natural planet (the Sun) and exit these spacesuits (the human body) and be united again as energy in heaven (the Sun). You hear them singing: "Walk in the Light".

~~

Now, just as the two barenaked wives and little Tifa departed towards the Nile River draped in their colorful beads, another woman, a young girl really, took a brisk walk to the compound where Kueth reigned.

She was called Nyatoot and was one of the tribal chief's twelve wives:

A beautiful girl with silvery charcoal black lavender skin and sheaths of knotted lion-like hair, all of the men in the village were in awe of not just her beauty, but also of the smell on her breath of other women. It was truly a great and dazzling mystery, thought the men, because they could not imagine, could not figure out, not even the animist wise men could figure out, how one woman could have the smell of so many other women contained so perfectly in her mouth. This magic trick made Nyatoot special and slightly feared.

She gyrated the innerball of her throat until the sound made one of Kueth's wives--Akinyi--appear in the entrance way and then Nyatoot asked to speak before him. Akinyi threw a light spray of moist sand on the girl's feet and announced her entry.

"Nyatoot! Is it you, the Chief's wife? With the sweetest promises of all your sisters wet upon your tongue?"

Nyatoot bowed down to Kueth as several of his children were gathered around his knees and inbetween his legs. Playfully basking in their Pappuh's affections. She told Kueth that she had come bearing a curse to which he immediately bed the children out-dawn to play.

Certainly, Nyatoot dare not reveal last night's haunting dream that had shown her the true face of Etah. Every man's beloved Etah. A vision so radical that her tribe might kill the messenger, just to be safe. So Nyatoot spoke not of it.

"A great cobra came down into the village before dawn", Nyatoot explained quickly. "It came as a curse to kill one of your wives I suspect, or possibly a child. But I heard it slithering down the center court of the village--and I put a bowl of breast milk from both my husband's wombbearers in front of the snake. And when her tongue tasted it, she spit out the afterbirth of a Hebrew sacrifice and withered into death."

"This is quite disturbing", said Kueth. "Who would want to hurt my family, I do not know. But what can I pay you?"

The vision of Etah had truly terrified Nyatoot. She had seen Etah's secrets and beliefs. Things that Etah would teach Tifa if the fruit was not lifted from the ground in time.

"Let me raise Soti's daughter", said Nyatoot. She reached with curled fingers inside the tight flesh of her woman's hole, wet and pink, and pulled out the head of the dead snake. She gave it to Kueth and requested, "I want only to raise the little one, Tifa. In this way, I promise, I can protect her. And she will learn magic from me and bring you a king-sized bride's price someday."

Kueth stared at her in contemplation. Then he said, "It

would move Soti to battle me. She is not of our people, you know. But what magic you know--I am curious to see."

Nyatoot rose up from the hard, packed ground and went to the earth between his legs. She knelt down and startled him at first by proposing, with quick body language, to take his manparts into her mouth. Eyes soft as Arabian silk, she calmed his alarm and did take him into her mouth. She did this until he became too afraid to continue it.

"Very well", Kueth told her with the hardness of a spear risen between his legs. "You may raise Tifa. But only to protect her. She is my child, my bride price, my earthroot."

Earthroot meaning heart.

~~

As the sun set and the moon rose and then sun and moon again, Etah returned entering the compound's great walls carrying little Tifa. But Soti was not with them.

Ofcourse not, thought Kueth. A bitter bileness rising in his chest; an eel's slippery membrane in his mouth. Soti's smile had been the sun. Her laugh, his favorite wine.

"Soti! My master, my husband--Soti was a witch!"

"No, no", protested Kueth. He wept bitterly, "A curse was placed on Soti."

Etah immediately bowed her head and said, "Yes, my wise husband. A curse."

Tifa, who was still terribly mutilated and blood-drenched from being cut between the legs, parted her lips but did not cry.

17

In Tifa's eyes, sunlight got tangled. Her taste hungered for bread and honey; her fingers longed for the black braids of her Isis doll, and in her body, she felt deformed and utterly raped.

Kueth, desperate to see Soti just one last time, clutched the sides of Etah's head with both his hands and kissed her very gently over both eyes. Instantly, he saw Soti's cranberry-Mediterranean complexion, dark and deep as mahoghany. Her beautiful face like that of a frisky leopard's. And her wrists bound together by a cobra. Beauty stolen from the majesty and wonders of Pharoah's Kamit. Escaping from purity. From him.

"I am glad that it is not a curse", said Etah. "Not a witch. So that she remains in the kiss of God's wife."

"Yes", said Kueth, unable to look at her, "...if she is properly sung after, kissed away and prayed for."

"I will do it", offered Etah.

Right then, two of Chief Bot's slave women appeared. Their lips stretched nearly to their bellybuttons with the heavy platewear that hung lodged in their subservient mouths. It was a wealthy society that could afford plates for the mouth of every slave. It is still said all these thousands of years later that Kamit (Egypt) envied Cush, but didn't want to copy.

"They have come for Tifa", said Kueth. "The girl, Nya-toot, wants to raise her. But I am no fool. It was Nyatoot who placed this curse on my sweet Soti. I will go to the Chief and reveal, once and for all...how it is that the smell of many women does honey the tongue of mysterious Nyatoot. She sucks the

the women out from the limb of a man's great tree, *that's how!"*

Etah bowed her head to show respect for his yelling. But of what he spoke, she knew not. So that come the nightlark, when the sky was purple and alive with insects bearing all the secrets of that millenium, she wept a great totem over Soti, and though silent, Tifa would always remember seeing her slain mother and thinking how she had looked like a sacrifice—vagina wide open, face cold and ashy, soaking in a pool of blood. Vultures lining up on a red clay earth. They had the same dark face, Soti and Tifa. They had been a mother and a daughter.

~~

White tree roots were dug up from the earth and eaten. The Nile gave plenty of fish and croccadile meat. Pregnant bellies either hung or stood straight out...decorated by the proud scars and markings that represented not just art--but what the individual's preferences were. It was a good season coming on, and although Kueth had planned on going to the Chief and revealing Nyatoot's wicked magic--Kueth's first wife, the lead wife who was called Hotemp--she rubbed his temples and spoke against it. "If you kill a witch", said fetchingly plump Hotemp, "it will only unleash all her jinns, her testimonials against us. Let Nyatoot be surprised in the bush instead. Your beloved Soti, I promise you, will find her there."

Kueth, filled angrily like a sack of red crabs, silenced himself and took heed of his wife's decree. And so it came to pass that Nyatoot was traveling in the sudd-forest one afternoon...her eyes searching for blue bees and honey ants...when a swift, horny hyena leaped laughing from the bush and ripped out her tiny young throat in one bite!

Now, however, Hotemp was very worried upon hearing it, because one would have expected it to be a *sexy leopard* leaping into Nyatoot's last breath. Why the horny hyena? Could it be that *Kueth* was the jinn to be feared?

She thought maybe so when the night came and Akinyi ran to her quarters to tell what she saw. The young wife said, "I saw our great husband with his hands clutching Etah's head...he pulled her down and put the branch of his great tree inside her mouth...like food."

Aha! figured Hotemp. That is it! Kueth had probably put all his wives *on the breath* of the Chief's favorite wife, Nyatoot. Thus the horny hyena silencing the poor girl before she could reveal that Kueth had raped her in the mouth. It all made sense now, thought Hotemp, as she tiptoed to the edge of a clay wall's sand-netting and peeked into Kueth's sleeping quarters. She saw the tree juice dripping from Etah's mouth and heard the irhala as they escaped from Etah's throat. Kueth's long legs were spread wide; the color of darkest ebony nightwater--shiny black as Etah--so that seeing them together, black on black, was like seeing the genesis of vision itself. Hotemp recoiled with jealousy.

"You feel honored?", Kueth asked Etah.

"Yes, my master, my husband", replied Etah.

"Good. Now go from me, beloved wife, and send me my lovely Mojooni." Dutifully, Etah bowed and backed out of his presence.

But later, in her quarters where she dismissed her slave and tendered her own infants, there were tears in Etah's eyes. She had not liked this new act, this new taste. She did not like it, as well, that Kueth and the Chief had appointed her as the adoptive mother for Nyatoot's children. But to protest or disobey...Etah would rather die first. Be stoned at the river!

Hotmep and Akinyi huddled over palm wine and laughed later that night. Hotemp declaring, loud enough to be heard, "She had her mouth full; obedient black Jew-bitch!"

~~~~

*T*wo thousand warriors flanked the walls of the village! For as far as the eye could see--blue black muscle, royal as the phallic sceptors of modern day Sudan, stood draped in flowing red robes of Arabian silk, golden tunics from kamit, emeralds and rubies encrusting every spear, every shield of croccodile husk. The royal emblem of Cush burning against youth's brow anointing honor, bravery and raw naked manhood.

Indecently innocent. Soft, earthly, naked and wet.

Naked and joined at the collarbones by chains of white pearl came the feminine glory of three hundred and seven *chocoLat*-skinned virgins, doe-eyed with seashells from the shores of Punt decorating their wooly hair. Awaiting the gaze of King Piankhy and his blessed nod of approval. This was life...at its sweetest.

Chocolat earth. Pretty rain and earth women; dancing.

Etah stifled her feelings as one of Nyatoot's daughters was given up by Kueth to be a slave offering--a virginal gift to King Piankhy. Little Tifa cried as they took Adusa into the hut of the plate doctor...for inside, an incision would be inserted. Over time, the slit would be increased and a larger plate added, then later a larger one, until the lip stretched and stretched into the magnificience of submission. But Etah did not show the sadness. It would be against the will of man to do so.

"It is Etah!", declared Kueth, "who is the *real* woman. And so, in my absence, she shall rule my household."

This was, for Etah, a great honor. But for his lead wife, Hotemp, it was nothing less than public humiliation. Hundreds of village women, even slave women, would laugh at her for weeks to come! She hung her head as Kueth handed Etah the most bejeweled spear in his house. He said, "I trust in you, Etah. With my very manhood."

A slave boy rose the stones of the threshold and clacked them together in unison with the bells on his feet. *For our God Piankhy! Keeper of the Kiss of God's Wife! Hai--hoodi!!"*

BOOF! came the drums.

A hundred white camels were pulled to their feet and great rainbows of flags rose as the people cheered!

Princess Bast...her golden thighs like wet lard in the

abdomen of honey ants...lifted her veil and showed the knots where her breasts had been cut off; cast into the Nile. She began to sing. To rub the fur of her woman's hole against the back of her elephant in a rythmic gyration that celebrated the ongoing virtility of King Piankhy's late great father--King Kashta. Fat, bald and honey-stained, Bast was every man's exotic fantasy, and as a virgin for life, the Chief chose her to honor cleanliness by suckling the toerings of King Piankhy's highest wife and symbol of Cushite purity, Queen Imaktmen.

The camels followed the elephants, smoke rising into the sky like blue, red, green...white and deep purple dragons. The chocolat virgins rising in a dance. Their feet and necks, bound in that collective chain of pearl, foreheads nodding in the motion of antelope, of gazelle...calling to the black branches of the great trees. Thin shards of pure gold dangling between the muscular cracks of their bulbous chocolate-nut booty; the tiny arc of their backs. The warm wet dew of their rythmic, flat stomachs:

Leap into the sun, zarpunis!...give the soul!...feed the drum. Come virgins. Come down in love and purity. This is your great day. For the kiss of God's wife.

Choco-lat earth. Pretty rain and earth women; dancing.

And *growing* from every scalp...the crown of our fathers.

~~

Cushite women...after the men and boys were gone, took their daughters to the Nile. Here is where Marawi, the Goddess

23

of Counting and true mother of Isis...her plump face and fat black arms, her hair worn as twisting eels...waited to celebrate by counting the bounty.

Etah supervised her co-wives and dunked both little Tifa and Joosi. She made no sad sounds, no heartbreak that Adusa was gone. But, indeed, she was heartbroken and needful of prayer...*and that is how her downfall began*...or as some feisty African women might argue--her true beginning began.

~~

Tall and black. Black as all black put together. Etah carried on her head a weaved papyrus basket of bread, fruits, dried fish, a little goat's meat. Her hips swung of the creed of African womankind—the sway like that of a pendulum or some blowing scarf; some elegant snake zig-zagging up the side of a sand dune. Parched, crusty overworked black feet. And the babyish chocolate feet of Tifa and Joosi ahead of her like boys would do (*to announce her as a mother*).

Under the full radiance of the sun, they marched along until Etah found her favorite spot. That place where a large, smooth rock, almost lavender, reached out over a tiny artery of quiet lime river. The sun spilling down like warm honey.

She put aside her basket and told her daughters, "Now let me teach you to pray...as my mother taught me."

Taking their hands, they knelt down, heads bowed, as one.

Now Etah remembered the words of her dead mother--

24

Queen Atu:

"At the end of the day of all deeds...our mother, at last, will speak up for us. Redeem us. Our mother, the Lioness...for she is the Sun!...will return to the earth as a great and vengeful fire against all who caused pain, suffering and heartbreak. She will burn eternally...against the flesh of these transgressors...stopping only...when they have known every inch times seven of what they inflicted. Here is the rock and the red dragon."

Etah continued from her own earthroot: "For the enslavement of Adusa, for the enslavement of my own slaves and all wives and children like us...every *man* shall answer unto the Lioness!"

Tifa and Joosi almost peed on themselves!

For of all the words they had ever heard, they had never heard glowing ones like these, nor had intellectual presence of mind enough to have even imagined such a possibility. Not even in their wildest childheld fantasies. It was blasphemous!

"Now in the time before my mother's mother's mother", Etah told the girls. "My mother said that woman and man lived in separated tribes and that they became very fond of one another, visiting to make bounty. And that we all came from the garden in the land called Punt. For like the lioness...it was the woman who did all the hunting, the raising of the children, the choosing of the penis. But no more. This new society--my mother said she did not know. But she blamed it on socializing

25

with the Arabs. The Arabs, you see, are the lost children of the kiss of God's wife (Africa). But they introduced the practice of slavery to the blacks. They joked about, as they still do now, our dark coloring, our sundrinking hair. They taught us to be selfish and turn away from the trees, the Sun and the river. That is why King Piankhy has vowed to snatch Kamit away from the Arabs; *the sand lizards!* We blacks have been removed from our true destiny a thousand times over...and rarely by our own feet. Of this world, we are the damned. Not a friend anywhere who would take us *as ourselves.*"

Leisurely, Etah thought of her seven sons then and saw them before her...dark and purposeful, their legs and chests strong like one of the great pyramids surrounding Piankhy's vast walled city of stone. Cushite hands raising giant honeyants to full catepillar lips, biting and suckling the drop of pure honey from her abdomen. *The sun, full and yellow...in their faces.* But Etah, being a woman, would not be there to rejoice in it.

"My mother", she told the girls, "was called Atu. Highest wife of a King, Nobar. I inherited her charcoal black skin but none of her beauty. And when Nobar died--she was buried alive--with her husband and all his belongings as was their way in that land. But because I was the daughter of a King, I was married off easily, regardless of my great height. She told me that above all else...a woman obeys her husband, protects his honor and all the laws of his land. All this and eternity, too...

under the lioness". Sadly, she told them, "Ours, dear daughters, is for the next world."

But in that moment.

Tifa felt herself being called in some way. Her child's face, small and round, soft as the inside of an infant's mouth--it blanched lightly. Her eyes filling with tangled sunlight. Not only had she listened. She had heard.

So after praying for Adusa's revenge, they returned to the village, and Tifa breathed deeply as two bumps made nipples.

~~

Joosi was the one who told *it*.

Innocently showing off to an older girl, Nil's daughter, Ponis, as they braided, down the backside, one another's hair.

And when Nil slapped Ponis's mouth and dragged her to Hotemp's lair, *it* was sharp enough to cut.

Hotemp said nothing to beloved Etah about Etah's "prayers". She had some of the children ask Tifa and Joosi carefully hidden questions, but Tifa was too smart to be purged. She went to Mother Etah and told her that she saw *purple rain* (the tears of Kenyaku's persecuted one-eyed son from the time before time began) in the air. With a simple grunt, Etah waved away Tifa by saying, "Whenever evil comes...let it come. In *this* world, the men will shape it."

~~

Hotemp squatted over a sand hole in the ground and

took a long hard shit. A sexy leopard watching from the bush-
-and Hotemp! They shared the same tensed cheeks (a smile).
They could both smell the wild she-funk of a tarantula,
menstrating.

"Sweet *dirty* bitch", whispered Hotemp to the sexy
leopard's swooning delight. "Sweet...*dirty* bitch." Hotemp dug
her big toe into the sand, deeper...and deeper. "Sweet..."

~~

So when the nightlark came and the purple sky was alive
with the wings of our ancestors, Tifa was awakened by the raw
pungent stench of sweating sudd leaves. Her dead guardian,
Nyatoot, would have called this weeping. A warning.

Tifa sat up from the warm furry ditch in the ground,
three feet deep, that was her bed, and raised herself up to pull
away the overhead netting so that she could climb out onto the
packed dirt floor of her hut. Bells attached to the netting jangled,
because children were not allowed to do this without the slave's
help, but Tifa yelled out that she was alright before going to
the crystalized salt vase that had belonged to Nyatoot and taking
from it a glazed Scarab necklace (the Nubian beetle that signifies
ressurrection for its bearer).

Alu.

Children, the dead ones--die often from bravery.

Knowing it was against Cushite religious law, she put it
on before having started her monthlies, and then boldly stated
before it was proper to do so: "I am the daughter of the Sun, the

daughter of Kueth. I am my husband's beloved; a servant under his protection and a comfort to his mother. Many sons does my husband deserve. I am daughter of the Nile--the daughter of Soti, the daughter of Cush and the daughter of the Kiss of God's Wife. Unto every man--I obey, and in purity, the next world shall abide me."

Unfortunately for young Tifa, Hotemp and Nil stood outside the hut hearing every last sinful word of it!

"Tongueless be the woman...who speaks without a man."

~~

Kueth, the greatest husband. He returned!

All his women greeted him in a single line singing, veils over their ears and white ash blanketing their black faces. On their bare nipples was dried honey and between their loins a restless quiver of manloved scar tissue. Kueth, they thought, was their master and other self. Their authentic self who loved them.

"Pappuh! Pappuh!", the children chanted upon his caravan's arrival. Uncles and eldermen, too old to have made the trip, presented elaborate quilts that they'd made detailing the stories of their lives. One featured the image of Prophet Ciisa (his enemies called him Jesus Christ) giving droplets of water to an old and lonely injured warrior while sag-breasted black onyx women bowed their heads in the background. Another told of Swahili (an Arab slave language) being forced upon the tongues of African slave children in the east.

Mother Etah, having the longest arms in the village, held out Kueth's bejeweled spear and called out across the Nile, the desert and the jungle with a piercing, "Aililililililili!" Kueth loved to hear any of his women ululate.

As his camel lowered to the ground and he stood up in front of his many huts and gathered family, he presented to Etah the beautiful hides of ten leopards and two zebras...and covered her whole face *with the palm of one hand*, mimicking the kiss of the sun. It instantly established her as new lead wife, but Hotemp did not wince or flinch. She had been laughed about for some time now and merely held her buttock cheeks tightly closed, biding her time. Kaos was hers to wield at any moment she liked.

Etah said to Kueth, "My master, my husband. My time with you may not be much longer...but you have given me much more glory than I ever deserved."

Did she know of her demise, wondered Hotemp?

"Don't speak foolishly", Kueth chuckled. "Your time with me is forever. That goes for all of you!"

All his wives cheered and began to ululate.

A new wife to replace his beautiful Soti was then introduced. She was called Leek and came humbly from a Hebrew tribe on Libya's far coast. Her flesh was colored cinnamon and her hair was oily, stick-straight spiderwebs—thus half the family took pity on her, being so obviously tainted with Arab blood. And the other half was impressed. Etah inquired and learned that Leek had already been properly cut. As well, Leek had only seven teeth missing, and for a seventeen year old raised on milk and honey, that was pretty good. Ofcourse, like most straight-haired people in those days, she was suffering from the Sahra desert's sand fleas (lice). Mother Etah knew a remedy, though.

"We must feast on a great and endless meal!", Kueth decreed. "for from the backs of these camels, I have untold treasures and gifts for all of you, my beloveds!"

Just then, Hotemp sent Nil's daughter Ponis to the great compound of the Chief. "Report to him everything I have told you. Etah and the girl Tifa. The both of them must be exposed to the Sun with the faces they've painted on. Go now. Hut-Hutt, child!"

Refrain:

The Nile River at dusk when insects come. And everything of the swamps hum with the flapping of BesBoohi's wings and blue black faces from old great Nubia and mighty Cush...remembering then; the charcoal black faces of today's tragic Sudan. Eventually, it is said, we are exposed to the Sun with the faces we have painted on. To the Lioness, say the zarpunni. *Tima.* As then. Our cowardly faces meaningless.

~~

End of Tunnel:

It was the earthroot that rumbled inside of Tifa that cool fateful evening. She had already been put down for sleep, but could still smell the pungent dung of the leaping fire and could just imagine her Pappuh's wives dancing and laughing around its glow. The wine on their breath making their eyes more mysterious and sensuous than the black lavender blanket of sky that floated over the palm trees like some exotic rug floating down out of Kamit; out of Pharoah's hands. The *faces*, however, Tifa could not reconfigure. Something was wrong and she sensed it, but did not dare rise from her dwelling. No. Tifa would save the powers she was weaving.

Chief Bot had sent down three griots!

Accompanied by ten Cushite warriors.

"What disrespect is being shown my property!?", demanded Kueth in a drunken state. "I won't tolerate the uninvited! My compound is my kingdom!"

"Dear, dear brother", spoke one of the Gods while bowing his head to Kueth, *only* because Kueth was rich. "Our great Chief has chant us whisper three questions unto the ear of your wife, Etah. You yourself being a God, Kueth. It pleases you, too."

Kueth nodded to Etah...and she looked to the griots with a complacent indifference on her brow. They approached her until she towered over the circle that was around her. They whispered three questions and Etah answered truthfully, because she could not lie to men.

The griots then told Kueth, with a look of great disappointment on their faces, "The Chief will see you in public meeting under the sunlight. Your wife, Etah...and the blooming girl, Tifa..."

Oh no, thought Etah. Not Tifa. She's just a baby!

Etah dropped her head as if the wind had been knocked out of her. She would have liked to have protested the fate of Tifa--but to speak against the will of men; Etah would sooner die.

After the griots explained to Kueth the crime in question, he merely laughed, kicked sand on their feet and assured them, as he didn't believe a word against Etah, that his wife would be redeemed in the Chief's eyes come tomorrow--and that he himself would whip the backside of Tifa until the lashes were deep enough to last her into old age. Tifa, as a bride of highest asking price, was now lost to him forever. No man would marry a woman who had *spoken* without a man. Not even her being a properly cut virgin could lessen this particular insult against any and all Cushite males.

~~

In the hut, Tifa clutched the scarab in her palm. She gulped hard and waited for the moment of her first flight; the day of her first *roar*. Tifa had listened to the trees, had bled in the river and had offered her breasts to the Sun--she was not afraid and had decided to create within herself--a woman.

Woman:

The day began as shade and lurking sun for Tifa as she

watched Chief Bot set free five slaves who had finished their slavery debts. One of them, in fact, was scheduled to become the Chief's son-in-law. But first, before any weddings, there was the business of Etah and Tifa, and in Tifa's case, she had recited wedding vows without a man. For that, feared Etah, they might stone the girl.

Etah realized that she herself would have to die that day. There was no doubt in her mind that she'd be executed. So without pretention and full of complacent grace, she climbed atop the stoning mosque in the center of the village and stood before Chief Bot. Her breasts bare until the Chief ordered that they be covered up. This, as in almost all ancient African societies, was the highest form of dehumanization and public humiliation for a woman. To have her breasts covered.

But Etah, ofcourse, did not care enough about herself to feel anything but comfort through obedience. So when Kueth had to cover her breasts and there was an audible gasp from the hundreds of clansfolk surrounding the stoning mosque, Mother Etah stood tall, her beauty suddenly visible in all its pathetic dedication, shiny *blue* as the splashing winged velvet of a black majestic raven. She was there...for Tifa to witness.

Only the Sun remembers where our mothers began. For out of that dark tunnel; that righteous, heavenly peaceful inner blackness where all life begins--all the faces come out painted the same and are beautiful in the sun. Mother Etah knew, you see, that she was there...for Tifa and Joosi and all the other children, but especially her seven sons...to *witness*.

Chief Bot instructed her, "Repent your prayers Etah. Repent your indecent thoughts and all will be forgiven."

Mother Etah bowed her head, and for the first time in her life, she heard herself say: "My master, my Chief...I cannot..."

There was an audible gasp from the onlookers!

"...obey you."

The men huffed, the women squealed in shock, children got lumps in their skinny throats! The Chief thought he'd misheard her and told her again--"You are one of the greatest women of your people, Etah. We cannot bear to watch you die. So you must repent what you said against your sons, against the foot of all men. You must say that you didn't really mean it...as I surely know that you couldn't have possibly meant it."

Etah simply said, "When evil comes...let it come. In this world, the men will shape it." Then she sank to her knees and wept aloud, "I am evil. I will not obey."

Tears.

Hot, wet heavy tears ran down the rich man Kueth's cheeks--because he had never realized just how much he loved this wife. He heard Chief Bot saying, "Because you are obviously possessed by evil angels, Etah--I will allow you to choose the way in which you leave from man's foot."

"Separate me, master", whispered Etah on her knees.

Thus the wives of Chief Bot covered their faces with veils.

Indicating that Etah would be killed instantly.

Warriors marched out onto the stoning mosque and grabbed the coal black arms of the tall woman, but in the most shocking village event in more than a decade--Kueth actually jumped against the warriors and actually fought them off with everything he had! He was a like a mad lion; caged and desperate! He begged the Chief to take the lives of all six of his other wives instead! Finally, they knocked Kueth out.

Chief Bot, who also had tears in his eyes, told the warriors, "Let us return her to the Nile...with the understanding that she will not be burried in the center of the village...which is the tradition of all lead wives. For she will not be burried at all. So my foot decree!--so let it be done!"

"*HariHoodi!*"

BOOF! came the drums.

Gaafar once said: "The stupid child is the majority."

In swarms and mobs, the clanspeople went to the river and watched in stunned disbelief as Etah--Kueth's wife, *Mother Etah!*--was separated, her head from the body, and then the body cast into the red soot of the Nile. It was the men who wept bitterly as her head was placed on a stick. None of the women, none of the children. Just the men wept like young mama-tit boys.

But all the way back to the village stoning mosque, the little children tried to scoop up Etah's footprints...into their palms.

~~

You protected this man.

A *fool* who stood on a hill and proclaimed, "It wasn't our fault we killed our own mother! She was black and damned! She wasn't pretty! She was possessed by evil angels! She was black and damned! We had no choice but to kill our own mother!"

You protected this man.

~~

Tongueless:

On the day that Tifa abandoned her people and their village, she wore Etah's shrunken head and Nyatoot's Nubian scarab around the collarbone of her soft cocoa shoulders as a double-powered necklace. Kueth, ofcourse, had no idea that his daughter had stolen Etah's shrunken head, and as well, he had no warning that she was leaving him behind.

The floor of Tifa's mouth was silky-sore and meatless, a jagged empty nub, and the roof of her mouth was a hollow temple now--and her teeth were like rocks without an ocean to crash against them, because the wetness was removed.

With her tongue cut out of her head for the crime of having spoken Cushite wedding vows without a man, and with her lower lip now being stretched into slavery's submission, Tifa no longer cared about having a father.

The plate belonging in Tifa's mouth lay smashed on the ground! Grain, lion's meat and dried fish. She stole them!

Hotemp spied the angry girl running away on the back of a camel with one of her father's newly freed slaves, a redskinned African called Achwil, their lives and the Sun ahead of them in the southeast--the land we now call Kenya.

But Hotemp didn't call for help. Didn't alert her husband's guards. She just watched Tifa and Achwil riding off into the sunset. The two of them; black as all black put together. And Tifa, so full of earthroot and determination.

King Nall once said: "A man is nothing but his mother's bet."

Kueth, the unloved father, understood that now.

"For she is the Sun", whispered Kueth soundlessly, his deep ebony eyes staring out from the shadows of his rich man's lair. He thought--*she's got Etah's head with her!* He thought--maybe she can use it better than Etah did...maybe that's what a daughter is for. Yes?

Queen Vashti (Soft and Yellow)

*Christian Bible/ Book of Esther (Chapter 1/Verse 12)

When they stoned our mother out of Ethiopia, her nipples removed and her tongue cut out of her head (for the crime of having disobeyed her husband's command that she open her hooni hoosi hole to all the Kings at his golden table)...we Africans hid our sweet mother in the blood Nile of Sudan; the gardens and the swamps.

Into the arms of her mother's clan (warrior Black women of old Cyrenaica), Vashti returned unto those from whom she had been raised up by. Her plump soul-sprung beauty, like sunshine and peach meat beneath a blanket of cascading dreadlocks; it was all gone by then. Tending sheep, she displayed no self-pity. Whatsoever. And our ancient mothers sang, *for the very first time*, this Nilotic Hebrew spiritual that speaks of woman's great worth (please recite it softly):

Khu-Sahu Sekhem...enam betonim
onu ta
ba
ja-selah, ja-selah...Khu Sahu...jabbok! pinon
Sekhem...oosay beulah; betonim, enam
onu ta
ba...Khufu-nori
tima Sekhem

this is the long train
to the redeeming
sin

this is the Black womb
the scarification--so holy. Disrespecting
her vision; so soft/melting softly

the redeeming sin being
courage

courage is the chariot that redeems us
in sin

O my beloveds. *Help me!* Forsake me not.

this is the long train
where upon you

I depend

African Evenings

Two magic fish
breaking the surface so silver and gray
A murky liquid smoke
In the lake

of a volcano

Sky of orange sands
Against the black hole they
climbed down into...and down
-ward deep

His tongue is like a bird--her mouth
is like a nest
Two miracles of mudd, chocolat dolphins,
One eternal grace/Our food
for the gods
Her head is the smooth black velvet eggshell
His soul...the Sperm Whale's lava

for they never want to be...apart

These two drumbeats...in the volcanic heart
Where time is timeless

And getting late

Boy
Magic

---

a love story

It happened all the time. Nuntandi got it in her head that she could order her own fate and even went and borrowed shoes from the village schoolteacher (she didn't want to wear the ones her Aunt Sula offered, because Sula was dying from what rural African men call *'the women's disease'*)...with which to defiantly walk towards that fate. Off to the city, off to the white women's favor room in a building in that progressive East African city, Nuntandi sojourned, a full days' walk, until she ended up in front of a municipal judge...told him she'd been raped and by whom...and then found herself; like so few young women brave enough to make such an accusation publicly...arrested and imprisoned.

"I demand", threatened Nuntandi's white lady, Helen Gator, "that something be done about this matter. If not, I will go to the regional assembly myself. The human rights of this poor girl have been violated! She was raped by her employer."

A Nyoro woman named Ijobi translated the white lady's words into a language that Nuntandi could understand.

Nuntandi's last name revealed that her father's bloodline wasn't of the same tribe of most of the decent families in this country. Her father was a full-blooded Acholi--considered a lower class breed of Africans known for their notorious lying, stealing, laziness and general unworthiness as human beings. In fact, it was a disgrace that Nuntandi's mother had lowered her status by marrying something so niggardly as an Acholi.

Pungent heat and a few flies whirled beneath the whirling blades of the courtroom fan. The judge's face looked like a charcoal kite under a white wig of thundering cotton.

"We have to check you for diseases", the Judge informed Nuntandi on that first day. "Not only that, but your employer is a very respected and well-liked man from India. We must make sure that you have not slandered his good reputation. Lock her up."

"Don't worry", said the white woman as Ijobi translated. "I will do everything I can to prove your case!"

Nuntandi, barely seventeen, merely stared at the 'out of place woman' blankly. Her crisp African hair and young, parched flesh were drenched in sweat, but in her deep eyes...there was a filled-in kind of warming. So optimistic and secretly triumphant that it could only be called, when residing in the barefoot gaze of a teenaged girl--*boy magic* (first love).

Six Months Later:

Helen Gator arrived at the women's dungeon (situated under the much larger men's jail) just in time to hear the loud protesting of Nuntandi's cellmates. Quickly, the white woman hurried down the damp, poorly lit corridor of stone, mudd and straw...her senses quite used to the stench of diarrhea by now, but her eyes never quite adjusting to the casual ricochet of resident rats or the sooty mudd-clay faces of women and girls who had been jailed indefinitely for nothing more than stealing a slice of bread to feed their children or for prostituting their bodies to *earn* that slice of bread...or for revealing that someone had raped them. One woman was even in jail for having written a poem that had angered soldiers passing through her village.

"Filthy rotten Acholi girl!"

"Nuntandi?", called out Helen worriedly.

"She stinks!", spat a cellmate. "Under the skin she stinks!"

"Rotting inside", remarked another woman who sat on the cot staring at Nuntandi with bolted, mournful eyes. Being a mother who had lost her husband, four sons and two daughters, she could only shrink inward to her bones and mumble, "...it's the women's disease."

Nuntandi stood off to the side, her legs skinny and

44

wobbly as knot-bones, her dark left arm showing a small trickle of flaking scabby-white sores, and her gums, whenever she spoke or smiled, white with a creeping paste. Helen realized that Nuntandi probably had AIDS, but the court had refused to pay for any tests, and not only that, they still hadn't began any proceedings whatsoever to have Ghandi Mephisto brought in on the charges of having raped his employee. Forget it.

At this point, Helen's only real goal was to get the girl released from jail and returned to her village. Certainly, the baby couldn't be born in jail, and until she accomplished her client's release, Helen Gator wouldn't be able to sleep at night. Helen took twenty cents out of her pocket and paid one of the cellmates to translate a conversation between Nuntandi and herself. She now faced the girl with that familiar caucasoid expression of deeply projected remorse and pity. "Nun-tawn-diii?"

"I want Kimba", Nuntandi told her from behind the bars. The girl's face, to Helen, seemed strangely bony-chic and *exhausted* by being--as if a vision cast in mudd. It seemed, still, that the poor thing was in love. Absolutely fueled by it.

"You find Kimba", Nuntandi told Helen for the hundredth time, resting her fragile hands over the protruding lump that was her pregnant belly.

"I went to your village", Helen began in frustration, fighting back the tears, but Nuntandi did not let her finish. The girl insisted, "If I am alive...then somwhere you'll find him.

Kimba Kamilhgo, my kabaka; Kimba who loves me."

Those tears escaped Helen's pale blue eyes causing Nuntandi to giggle. Astonished by the tears and amused, she told the 'out of place woman', "Don't cry. You haven' t found him yet."

Then the woman on the cot, the older one who had lost her family to AIDS and whose hair was straightened and wild and whose face looked like a monkey's face with deep, dark ritual markings in it, looked up at the white lady and told her, "Go look in all the sinful, sordid places. The kind of places where your Jesus Christ would go. In the company of death, it would be far better that you bring the girl's boy magic...than to waste your out of place...space."

Death Comes to Children:

Nuntandi lay on the cot where the women tried to keep her bones and flesh from shaking. Her brow, as it sweat, they wiped it, and when she lost vision at times...they forgave that she was the daughter of an Acholi and held her crispy head of hair in their laps and sung her traditional songs that her mothers and grandmothers had known and sang. It was made all the easier for the women to comfort the young girl this way...because of the crazy smile that seemed as a ritual scar on the young girl's face. A foreign tongue.

"What dialect is this?"

"He came in the cassava season", Nuntandi whispered at times. Her sight failing and the light trapped inside her heart and lungs shining over bare, inheld reflections of the tall, very black and beautiful young man called Kimba. His African man's ivory smile and all the power of his collected family's eyes suddenly encapsulating Nuntandi all over again. She had felt so tiny that day...flashes of heat covering her flesh in deep wavey cowlicks everytime he looked at her.

"She's speaking in 'Makkutandi'...her mother's tongue."

"I worked in his uncle's garden", Nuntandi whispered to her cellmates in the hopeful darkness. "The garden of Ghandi Mephisto. And when he came to his uncle's altar after fighting the revolution--he found me in the sun. I was covered in sweat and had my basket over my head and neither my feet nor my breasts were covered as a christian's. And he liked it, the way that I had shaved my head and marked Kabaka Sengendo (a river God) virgins around it in white dots. I got water from the pond for him. And he had an illness about his bones, but he was the most beautiful thing that I had ever been looked at by. He drank it. He drank it down as if no girl had ever gotten him water before. Said his mommysweet had named him Kimba."

Black able hands tucked the raggedy blankets around Nuntandi's trembling body and began praying for the unborn. A light humming of song. For the baby.

But the bars of the jail could not hold Nuntandi back. She was out and beyond the will of her fate. Dancing. Covered over from head to toe. Picked up and moved. And someone saying, "This baby could be Jesus Christ coming back!"

Walk In the Light:

"I wanted to be a dancer", mumbled Nuntandi as sleeping sickness burst center-link in her giggling.

In her village, she had already been not only a dancing queen, but one of grace, agility and born genius. So good, in fact, that she had wanted the world to know it and had determined, rather bravely, that she would decree her own fate. So she had wrapped her body in her finest tye-dyed goddessa gowns, adorned her neck, wrists and ankles with all the trinkets she'd ever made, shaved her head, painted on the virgins for luck, hoisted a basket atop her head and sojourned by foot, a great distance south, to the bustling city of Kampala. For in Uganda's capital, she would find the famous African Makkutandi Dance Troupe of Kenya...and after seeing her audition, Nuntandi knew, they would be quite and utterly *impressed.*

Not only that, but she wouldn't have to worry about the stigma of being the daughter of an Acholi tribesman. It was well known that no less than three full-bloodeed Acholi females were featured dancers in this most celebrated of African dance troupes and that they regularly performed in places like Europe, Italy and Sicily, Japan and the United States. Why with her talent, youth and beauty (in that order), Nuntandi realized that she would become a star instantly! So off to Uganda she ran.

On the way, she met other disobedient young girls. Some whose dreams were even bigger than hers, but unlike her, they were neither brave enough nor smart enough to be stars, Nuntandi had realized. They were mere prostitutes swarming the dirt roads and bushens like packs of well-trained but hungry dogs. With dirt-ashy black and chocolate complexions straining beneath chalky makeup that was created to flatter the out of place women (not Africans)--they called out Nuntandi's gaze with a certain wildstankpussy--scented silence. Intelligence and girldreams stampeding through their heads like new breeds of animals unwelcome in Africa's traditional jungle. Plenty of spit and sperm covered them, because they had no fathers, and that's what they smelled like. Hope and wishes.

*The whites of their eyes had turned canary yellow...*and the black velvet of their skin was like a carpet ripped up, oiled and dirtied, then shampooed. They reminded one of coarse purplestank goodsmoke marijiana or evil black Halloween cats or butt-ugly (*OOuh-yeah!, mom*) AIDS-infected little African whores with Eve's bad skin or the current father's bad hair. Nuntandi, in all her snobbish superiority, accepted their directions, their protection and their food. After all, it was she who would redeem them. So she behaved as a grand princess and took everything they gave--as if they were low enough to owe it.

She had no idea that almost all of these girls were

orphans....not of the revolution. But of the *epidemic.*

"Wake up, Nuntandi...come to mama! Your baby!"

"Nun-tawndi? It's *Helen.* Helen Gator from the Women Standing Up for Women Center, hon!...why is she giggling so?"

"It's her mother's tongue she's speaking. Speaking of becoming a woman. Aii--boy magic! Ah!"

Own Me Night:

Kimba was like most of the world's men. He took pain away from the women that he cared about. He healed them. And from the moment he laid eyes on Nuntandi--he had noticed the bare-boned loneliness of her heartbroken silence. Her eyes held no illusions about courageous womanpride or independence, she was like a newly lost scarf on the wind. Her deepeyed African beauty softly brimming with an eager submissive vulnerability that is forever to the male human what lioness urine is to the mightiest of lions. *Irresistable.*

He did not know that she had danced like a spirit fashioned of part scarf, part wind and all eternal fire on that grand stage of the African Makkutandi Dance Troupe of Kenya...or that they had applauded her wildly, cheered her ecstatically...*and then held up* beside the complexion of her glowing face--*a manila envelope,* of which Nuntandi was obviously darker, and for that reason alone--would not be allowed to join the troupe. This time, it wasn't her tribal heritage, but her black beauty that disqualified her.

It made no difference that every male dancer in the group was two buckets blacker than her or that she could out-dance all of those beautifully exotic females that were light as burnt orange clay. What mattered, the Monsignor explained to her, was that in front of rich African males and all foreigners abroad...a lighterskinned, less African-looking dancing girl was more acceptable, media-marketable and less provocative. Even on tours in the West Indies and amongst Black Americans...the cover version was preferred over the original. And out of hurt and anger, that's just how Nuntandi saw herself--as the original; the authentic black woman. The *real power.*

But Kimba had not known why she was heartbroken that first day in his uncle's garden. All he sensed was that she needed him, and being needed is a condition that men like.

He had approached her with simple caring. As if men and women could be nothing less than great comrades. That's how he courted her, each and every day, in the garden of Ghandi Mephisto.

They swirled their feet in the pond and spoke about the revolution while Nuntandi fed him flakes of tofu and slit-open roasted yams with plant's milk and ground cinnamon. She learned of his tens of thousands of brothers who had lost the war. Their reflection being his own. She learned of the nightmares that tossed him up at night. His memories going back to cutting off hands and ears, kicking in the doors of begging mothers, shooting men dead and burying children who had fallen under the might of green metal elephants. He told about poking the wives of his captured enemies, drinking swamp liquor and pissing on a portrait of Moga Davi right after helping to overthrow the bastard. He revealed to her, by telling his experiences, that he needed healing.

However, she already knew, instinctively, that Kimba's wounds were far too deep to be healed by something so pure and natural as what she felt inside herself for him. Feeling for him made her feel like a woman. Or atleast she felt like what she'd been told a Basotho woman was supposed to feel like over the prospect of being chosen by a man to whom she may now shower with love, obedience and unyielding subservience. If she couldn't be of a lighter complexion or of a more powerful tribe, then she could atleast be a good wife.

One day...Kimba rubbed his nose on her nose, and Ghandi Mephisto saw them and called his nephew onto the patio and rebuked him. "This girl is a servant and a runaway! Poke her in the bushes and leave her there, young lion."

The sky was a soft majenta blue that day with burning lava in the cloud slits faraway. Vultures circled an ailing brown fawn in the bush miles away. Nuntandi overheard Kimba saying, "She's a virgin, uncle. She's not stupid or common or selfish. Nuntandi is young and *willing* to be loved...and I love her. Nothing can compare to her."

In Kimba, Nuntandi knew about fire. Like a cat that

52

leaves its master before he dies, she could smell the illness about his bones, but had not a clue that it was stronger than him. For it seemed that nothing on earth was stronger than Kimba. Nothing taller, wider, blacker or stronger. Kimba.

I love her!

Twisting the godberry; he got the juice on his fingers.

Cheap Italian Disco Music:

Evil angels swept down from eternal white clouds, and despite all the long unmentioned love between Africans, it was the white cloud and the beauty that hides her face that slithered its cool tongue down the spine of Africa's bewildered, the three-legged, who were traditionally unkempt in the glaucoma-eyed stare of obedient wives and dark relations who historically have beat a drumbeat of false communication. *Here--line up for your injections.* With every breath, the sleeping lions fell upon their swords. Black masks reduced to white ash---a white crab munching at the follicle of pubic hair while the blood beneath dead skin itched of freedoms, seeping and ignorant, adjoining this band of angels. Like a heavy syrup, the sun poured her feminine darkness over the eyelids. Then the white men packed up their cameras, their monkeys and their legions...of flies.

Enschalla-amen.

Once a love is cast, it cannot die, but *wither* to bloom again. Each human being...being that love. For we twist the godberry, our throats in a mighty thirst for God's juicy promise. We all, collected together as humans...are the ritual that needs to be quenched.

She needs me to love her!

Fuck that monkey-bitch in the bushes and leave her there!

This is not India, Uncle Ghandi. This is Africa. Her black-berries are needed here--she belongs!

Spoken as if...you need her...to love you.

Could we ever have ourselves to ourselves?

Africa stinks like a dying whore!

But...to wither no matter, Uncle. For she is the one thing that can grow...unwatered. Africa.

Like a field of weeds.

But if she is a weed, then she is...MY...weed. The Goddess Flower. The mother of my whole being, my own reflection--that I love more than any other. And will not cut from time's heart!

Mother Africa:

Orange fire in a trash can at early dusk as the white bottoms of charcoal black feet danced in spasms, their heels beating against the brown earth that sustained them. This is where Kimba left his mother. NunTezu. Her memory and the one before she was stoned to death.

"Return to me", she once whispered. The great mass of her lips, all the syrup inside them, kissing at the middle of his soft forehead and gently over the eyes. "Return to me."

The nipple entered his mouth and then his belly filled with milk and honey...and good African music with which to grow a lingering soul.

Or draw colored figures on flesh and mask with erect African fingers...like mothers lingering.

NunTezu had a way of staring at Kimba. A way that the other mothers did not have, because in her secrets, she knew that he was not her son, but a miracle.

The white men had handed him to her just as they handed over all their miracles:

She had been weeping profusely. Her boy had been playing with other children when a hyena leapt out of the bush and got hold of his little arm.

Dragged him dead before NunTeza could get there.

Young Kimba, just seven, had died from a bite to the skull before she could get there and cradle his head and whisper the magic words, "Return to me".

"Ten dollars for your son's body", the white scientist had said. "Ten dollars, NunTezu...and I'll bring him back to life."

Blue eyes are like windows to an impotent paradise.

So NunTezu watched the out of place men carry her dead son's limp little body back to their mysterious compound, and NunTezu's husband took the ten dollars against her wishes, and they never burried their son and NunTezu refused her husband sex--forever after.

No men, NunTezu knew, had the power to bring the dead back to life. Only our wombs, she thought, has that power. So again she had whispered, "Return to me."

And then four years later--she saw a little black baby playing in the compound's yard. It was her son! Only he was a little baby again! In the yard of the White scientists.

Born all over again! Living again! The baby even caught NunTezu staring at him, but didn't seem to recognize her. With a wobbling head, large curious eyes and a drooling mouth, he just stared out to his original mother. Seeing her.

NunTezu could not believe it. The white men had brought her dead son back into his body, starting all over from the beginning, alive again!

Her reaction was to steal the boy and run as far away to another country as she could get.

And that's just what she did.

"No, not Edward. That's not your name. Your name is Kimba. Say eeet...Keeeem-bah!"

"My name...Kimba! Kimba my name."

Like a great, beloved egbo tree, he grew tall and black right before her wet sparkling eyes. Until he was taller than. Until the smile in his mother's very black pretty face seemed as sacred as the half-moon in a purple-black jungle sky.

Until the revolution came and they were hungry and looked down upon, because NunTezu was a single mother (which is freakish), a foreigner, and she stole food to feed them...for which she was stoned to death.

Lonely man-hungry thief!

She should of went back to her own tribe!

"When I saw Nuntandi's face and her bare breasts and the way that her head was smoothly shaven and beaded just like a princess--her eyes looked up at me--and in their lonely darkness I heard *'return to me'*...and I did not...look away."

"He is Kimba who loves me."

"I never tire...to watch her dance. For me, she laughs."

Kimba and Nuntandi:

The baby's fingertips were tiny as boiled rice pods and the face would have been Kimba's exact, thought Nuntandi. She wasn't surprised that he came out dead. Covered in an orange goo, skin like rubber, stinking. Born dead.

"I want", said Nuntandi as she began to cry, "...to die, too. This is not of a natural world. Not out of the love we made...this shouldn't be the result. We gave only purest love."

Helen Gator nodded sorrowfully after it was translated.

"Don't worry", Helen said through her own tears. "We'll find a happy ending for you." White-like like that.

And then two days later...Nuntandi was released from jail and quickly diagnosed with AIDS.

To which she responded, "I am not afraid."

"Tell her that...that I have bad news about Kimba. He's not coming back for her." The lady translated.

"No", said Nuntandi calmly. "He's waiting for me. I can *feel* it. Kimba who loves me."

"He died shortly after he left you at his uncle's compound, Nuntandi. From AIDS."

"No", she whispered through a cracking voice as her face creased with devastation, at last. Defeat bracing her dwindling frame. Her eyes virtual whirlpools of tears. She moaned out like a wounded animal, wretchedly, "...Kimba who loves me!"

I'm In the World:

Each weekend, Helen Gator donned her widest straw hat and went to the makeshift AIDS camp; rickety shanties of the Cawie plains where the sick and dying could rest safely without danger of being beaten in the streets, thrown into rivers or set on fire by embarrassed family members. This was where Nuntandi turned eighteen one humid afternoon. Her face of black velvet and deepeyed African beauty wasted away until it was so small and shrunken that it could literally fit into the cusped hands of a child. Out of kindness, someone had preserved her African dignity and femininity by shaving her head and decorating it with the images of the river ancestors. Helen Gator, the out of place woman; the white man's mother, *kissed* her on the forehead each time she came.

"Happy birthday, Nuntandi."

Someone translated for Nuntandi. Then they told Helen about the white men scheduled to arrive that day. Reporters with television cameras from America. "To show how sick and pathetic we are. The camp warden here is lining up the bleakest, blackest, ugliest of the wasting and all the children, like legions of flies--so their disease can be photographed first."

"They never show our grand cities", snorted a rather healthy woman; one of the nurses. "They never show us in church or in our seats at university. They never show our elaborate wedding ceremonies or the fathers teaching the boys to hunt, the mothers teaching the girls to weave. They never show the contest between the homes--to see who has the oldest warrior mask on the wall. Our great legacy of unkillable Kings and Queens, our great civilizations. No, no, white lady. They come to show our death. As much as they can film it. To make us so pitiful and lowly that our children won't want to be like *us* anymore. They want to show themselves, their white hands, giving us food and medicine. Their bloody white hands. They want to show that we are the pollution of the world--when it's really *your people* who are. They want to make our children ashamed of us and hate Africa. Want to be white or be like the niggers you created. And return no more. But every night, my husband tells our son...'*return* to me!"

Helen didn't know what to say. She simply nodded politely and took a seat next to Nuntandi's cot. She was glad to see the huge smile on the girl's tiny face as she handed her several birthday gifts--a new pillow, a new bowl, *baby powder!*, a beaded necklace from the village craftswomen.

"You are...a very kind white lady."

"It's nothing at all between sisters", Helen said holding Nuntandi's hand. "I'm just so sorry that you were stuck in that horrible jail for so long. I consider it my fault."

"But white lady. Nuntandi says in her language...'It's O.K. I've been in prison all my life'."

"Oh really? Where at?"

"Nuntandi say...'*wherever I was*'."

Signature of the Illicit:

"Soon", said Helen. "I must return to America. There is an election going on and I must help Bill Clinton defeat George Bush. I will be gone at least six months, Nuntandi."

The translator deliberately kept this from Nuntandi. She told the girl something else and then translated the reply. Helen removed her crucifix necklace and offered it as a goodbye, but Nuntandi refused it. Waved the thing away.

Nuntandi spoke, her eyes watching God.

"Sometimes I am so happy. When my eyes are *closed*...I begin to dance and I'm in the world. I'm in the world. I have my admirers watching on and Kimba has returned to me. And my baby not dead. He a boy. Boy magic. Alive and well and calling for me to come put him on my back and take him across the river. Like all the mothers before me. So he can be a man one day. Like his father. Like my father. Like *your* father. Sometimes, I am so happy. So happy that all I can do is dance, because this is happiness to me, to dance."

"You know...the television crew has asked the warden for permission to interview you on camera. One of the producers walked by and noticed how you are always smiling. This will make you a big star in America!", cheered Helen. Her hands were clasped together beneath her chin, her pearly white teeth glistening. So here she was...out of place and strangely naive. The white man's mother.

To which a stunned and diminishing Nuntandi quietly advised: "If you truly believe in God, then be careful not to brag--for if God observes that you are strong enough to take a bullet--then surely, he will arrange for you to be shot. That is the way of all Gods...Hell-in. I don't do *interviews*."

The character "Nuntandi" is portrayed on the front cover of this book.

Black America *Diva* GIRL:
black america/DIVA
girl

~~~

Victory and optimism precede daybreak for the people of West Africa, lately. Everyday. It seems that Senegal and Ghana are not only stable, but progressive. Nigeria, Africa's recently corrupt and ugly beast, is settling back into its classic majesty of old. For only the West Africans can boast of such great expectations, such health and harvest. It is as if Olorun and Olakun have weaved a new laimomo. Life is good and hard and difficult, yet bursting with blooming bright colors and ivory white smiles in this seafood mecca, the city of Port Wolofu.

"Big see-stuh! It's me--Alice! May I come in?"

Stick-figured, wide-eyed, devilish Alice at the latchkey!

Orisha Diop, pregnant with her husband's third child, opened the door...immediately embarrassed by what Alice had on. Orisha clutched at the crucifix that hung around her neck.

"Enter at once, babysister."

"Hello!", cheered Alice.

"Did people see you come up to the gate like that?"

"Like what?", teased Alice. "Black America Diva girl!"

"For all and sundry", whispered Orisha, frowning. Then she instructed: "Well go on. Have a warm seat, Black America diva girl. I hope your bottom doesn't get cold. Or splintered."

~~

Orisha poured them tamarind juice while Alice was already stuffing Lalo fruit between her sensuous beestung lips--which were painted a shocking majenta cr'eme, *silver* in the middle!

"Comes around was father."

"Our father--here in the city? Today?"

"I didn't tell him about your acting out."

"I haven't been bad at all, Isha! Stop bullying!"

"Look at you, Alice! I don't care what you do--you will never look like a black american woman."

"Correction", snapped Alice, her eyes flashing arrogantly. "No matter what *they* do--they will never look like *moi*!"

Orisha rolled her eyes and waved away a big, black fly.

"I'm tired of your cruelty, Orisha. You think every girl who isn't like you is a bad girl. But no. I don't want to be a pregnant cow! I don't want to be married to a black horn-frog who jumps on every lean, giggling schoolgirl between here and Congo. I don't want to sojourn to market with a basket on my head--I *needed* that automobile. Old government men..."

"Enough!", shouted Orisha as she leaped into standing position (imitating a man ordering respect from an unruly child or female in his house).

"My husband's indiscretions are beneath my grace!"

"You're just like Mother. A long-suffering black pathetic coward."

Tears swelled in Orisha's eyes as she demanded, "Then what would you have me do to Tiju-Iku, eh? Tell me wisdom!"

"Stop loving him!", answered Alice, swiftly. "Get father to have his legs broken...his memory changed. Then leave him with flies swarming about his jungle-knotted head!"

Orisha cried scornfully, "You hate men! You hate them!"

Alice burst out laughing. "I don't hate men, Isha! I *owe* them. Every woman does." She gulped down her tamarind juice before lighting up one of those godawful cigarettes.

"Father would be disappointed in you."

"Ofcourse he would", acknowledged Alice, blowing smoke. "But if you keep your throat dry and change your memory--he won't have to know."

Orisha shook her head as if in the presence of Favor Lady or a prostitute. She said, "You know how father is. We girls, the three of us, are his beloved totem, his shield of pride. Not one of our five brothers is treated with the rare favoritism that father bestows upon us...and this is how you repay him, Alice. By sleeping with dirty old men who run the government and getting private use of a publicly rationed automobile. This is how you honor father's name; unmarried and no longer a virgin...dressed as a carryabout, never once attending church services this year!...your *hair*, singed like some black american woman imitating a European. What is next? Blond dog hair and blue eyes imported from some caucasoid laboratory!?"

Alice gulped with guilt. Parliament Rector Karamoko had just ordered her a pair of blue lens eyes, fully paid for.

"Every night...I pray for you, Alice. That you regain your sight and come, with your tail between your legs, to Christ."

Orisha had just called Alice a *bitch*--in dignified African fashion.

"I don't need the white man's gutter religion", replied a heartbroken Alice. "But...I need my big see-stuh's understanding."

Orisha, her head wrapped in a towering fabric of beautiful sapphireberry and her peanut butter colored fingers gently dangling a crucifix--looked only at the floor.

In tears, Alice left just as Orisha's children returned hungry and excited from schooling. When neither of them gave a greeting or called Alice 'Aunt', her tears turned to loud sobs and she ran down the street...like a wet dog.

~~

"In Jesus name I pray", whispered Orisha on her knees, "Amen." Then she opened her eyes and rose up from the floor. She opened the dresser drawer next to the bed and pulled out a doll that represented the body of her husband, Tiju-Iku. Lightly, she kissed the smooth dark brown belly of the carved wood and breathed in the scent of the tiny cotton clothes that were made from old scraps of Iku's actual clothing. For even the doll's hair, thick and wooly like an African rain forest, was taken from Tiju-Iku's head.

And in it she had weaved strands of Yaro and Vashti's

hair. The children. Sweet, chocolate-faced angels who lay fast asleep now after enjoying yassa chicken and a game of checkers with their mother. Their hair, too, was weaved about the doll's head--so that Orisha could protect them all.

Orisha got into bed, holding the doll close to her, and tried not to think about Tiju-Iku's not being there. Or the fact that he was with some other woman and probably wouldn't be home until very, very late. She closed her eyes, and without sleeping, drifted back to her childhood. Back when her heart and mind had been like an unfinished fairytale waiting for this marriage, this man, this bed and this love inside her--the happy ending to arrive. Her belly had been like all the other young girls, full of butterflies, their collected dreams and the glistening cooked chocolat shoulders of dust-headed young boys churned up together under the heavy syruped sun's orange-red kiss. Like frightened does over a cliff--little girls with eyes as deep as all the cooked chocolat in the world had dreamed of crashing into that hot yellow center in the sun...that passionate eternity of lifestorms, mother-myths and children singing. Only a man could take you there, promised the moon at night.

So now Orisha was there. Holding her doll. Drifting off to sleep--only to be awakened by Tiju-Iku.

"Eww...what time is it?", she mumbled coming awake.

Tiju-Iku kissed her on the mouth and she could smell palm wine. His skin was hot. He got atop her and spread her legs apart, and as they spread, her heart was like an oyster's shell being opened and spilled light that had been lonely. Iku's bare chest came down against her own until the crucifix between her breasts was smashed between a furnace of heartkissed skin; cooked chocolate and peanut butter. Mr. Diop was poking inside her and declaring in the Wolof language: "I love you, my woman! I love you!"

He stopped abruptly. He rolled off sweating---smelling like the fish vendor's niece, Akosiba. But when a man has gifted you with his children and done backbreaking work in the shipyard all day, a good wife does not sour him.

Orisha's lonely light crept back inside its shell. Her body, which had been on the verge of warmth, was suddenly like wet flesh having its cozy towel yanked away! That quick.

"I got you a gift", said Mr. Diop, tiredly. On his back, panting with his eyes closed, he handed her a paper sack he'd brought home.

Orisha forced herself to smile, to act giddy and happy. But when she opened the bag, she was disappointed and confused. Inside the bag was one of those chemical boxes--the kind that were popping up all over Africa in the last fifteen years. Before that, only rich African women were familiar with these chemical boxes.

Orisha asked, "Why did you bring me this?"

"To straighten out you hair, figure it easy. And it's the expensive one, too. Took me three months to save for it."

He looked at her. His eyes awaiting some great gushing

excitement and joy. "...welll?"

"But you've always loved our hair", she replied. Recalling the passionate history of Africa's great lovers, without even knowing it, Orisha stated, "In one another's hair...we have always played. Remember? It's our father and mother's crown? The *proof.*"

"But this is the modern style, little yam! All the rich men's wives are enjoying it. All over Africa! Luckily, you already have sunlight in your skin. But now--your hair can be straight."

Orisha frowned and hung her head.

"But what's wrong with the hair that God gave me!?", demanded Orisha, angrily.

"God gave you a man's hair", Tiju-Iku told her, convincingly. He said, "I talked to my boss--and he says it's not feminine for our women to be walking around like this. Looking like men."

Orisha was aghast! "But you never thought I looked like a man before. You never ever complained about our hair. *Our children have our hair!* God's gift to us, the crown that he put only on one great and mighty people! It's what makes us unique from any other. You used to say it yourself. African hair! Anywhere in the world that you find it on someone's head, of any color, any race--it is the proof! The crown!"

"It's just *you*!", Tiju-Iku enthused, taking her hands into his. "You, the women. It's time to look more modern. More appealing."

"Like a European woman?", Orisha hissed as a single hot tear of betrayal ran down her left cheek.

"Don't insult me, Isha! I'm not some wish-I-was white Black American niggerman! I'm not..."

Orisha threw the box in his face! Then she got up and informed him that she was sleeping on the floor in the livingroom. She reminded him that her father would never speak to her with her natural hair mutilated in such a degrading fashion.

"But you married me!", yelled Tiju-Iku. "I'm your father now!"

~~

Unlike so many naked black women in Port Wolofu who only claimed to be beautiful...Alice Maissa was the vision itself. Her baby-soft skin was creamy rich like chocolate pudding and her eyes sparkled with a wickedly innocent precision. She had hoonta bonbon brown eyes (the happy chocolates), classic African cheekbones (she called them *Indian* after seeing an American black woman on circuit telelvision claim it) and the sexy bellpepper-thick flat, wide nose of her race. Large, pungent catepillar lips...and her hair, chemically straightened, hung around her shoulders like a black velvet cape. Her toothpick body featured a stunning, swinging bushwoman's bubble-butt and small perky breasts that were common enough in these parts, but with a perfect gap between her two front teeth--she definitely qualified as the traditional image of Pan-SeneGa world class beauty. In fact, the only thing she lacked...was a circumsized vagina and her hair plat-dragged.

Parliament Rector Karamoko gave her a good hard slap across the ass and then clenched her buttocks tightly in his big, wrinkled elderly hands.

"It is your ass to slap", Alice giggled, born naked, as her coal black areole jiggled with jolly. She was glad there wasn't much more he could do to her--being so old and limp.

"My son has a son", he told Alice, suddenly. "He's a good boy. Yassoungo. He just became a captain in our nation's airforce. While his wife was busy tending their newborn, I showed him a photograph of you."

Alice knew in her gut that a married man from her nation's rag tag airforce wouldn't have any significant money. Maybe a little power--free passes, minor authority.

"I'm giving you to Yassoungo", Karamoko announced. "He'll be coming to town once a week. I'll arrange for you to keep your apartment, ofcourse. Girly...what's wrong?"

"Nah-theeeng", she sighed, heavily. Soon she would have to endure a very large penis from Yassoungo, probably. Drats!

Karamoko reached over to the nighttable. He took from it a book that he had written many years ago during the revolution that led to his country's independence. A book that had made him world famous, entitled *"Africa for the Africans: How Europeans Raped Mother Africa."*

He took the hardback book and asked Alice to read the name on the cover. She answered, "Henry karamoko."

"And who is Karamoko, my child?"

"One of the founding fathers of this great country", she replied after having been coached so many times.

Pleased with her answer, Karamoko then gripped the book with both hands and whacked Alice across the forehead with the front of it! He asked, "What's that?"

"A book you wrote", she whimpered.

He whacked her across the forehead again. "What's that?"

"A book you wrote!"

"And why are you so grateful to share this bed!?"

"Because of your greatness, founding father!"

Whack!

He did it again and again until his penis became erect. And then, once achieving erection, he stared at it for the precious seconds before it softened and returned to being like an ashy black worm in a wrinkled patch of elderly white, yellowing hair. For Alice's participation and patient cooperation, he had been most grateful.

~~

Pira PookBu was one of those beautiful but rare half-caste women in Africa; the daughter of a Wolof African soldier and a White Dutch mother whom everyone in town secretly called "Favor Lady", because, according to Tiju-Iku: "She has this attitude that her presence here is doing us Africans some kind of favor. Just watch her long enough--she can't wait to show you her privileages. She can't wait to prove that her heart is just as African as yours--or that she, because she's the media's epitome of everything good and right, influences exactly what you feel and think. She wants to dance in your hut until your babies are pale with confusion. She's the white man's mother, the Favor Lady, the superior white bitch-rat who bequeaths our dirty little African children a favor just by being here--ungodly eggeating skank! Thank God there is no slavemaster here in Africa to declare that one drop of our precious African blood admitts *just any spoonhead* into our ranks."

Pan-SeneGa men always cheered this in-house sentiment, but held in silence--was the the fact that Tiju-Iku often used the image of Favor Lady as a vehicle for his own masturbation, his own secret *black devil-dog* desires.

Tiju-Iku's racist words aside, Orisha and Favor Lady's daughter, Pira Pookbu, became the very best of friends. Inseparable, in fact, and Pira, who was very beige colored with cascading wild tendrils of hair, never acted as if the two of them were any different from one another. Pira's brother, who had married a Dutch girl and moved away to London, was a different story. He hated his father's race and could make racist jokes with the lowest of the Dutch, French, English and especially Portuguese, but Pira was not one of those half-castes that acted superior, all and sundry and whatnot. Like Orisha, she was a proper housewife and a good christian and casually remained mostly African.

Together, the two young wives walked down Ipaboh's orange dirt road, draped in long flowing boubous of sapphireberry blue, carrying baskets filled with materials atop their heads. Orisha was a dollmaker and Pira made the most inspired of Ashanti-like quilts, her husband being an Ashanti-rights lawyer.

Suddenly--up ahead--orange dustclouds filled the air! A leftover Mercedes Benz, official car of Africa, was coming towards them, parting all the colorfully dressed headwrapped women and the swarms of playful, nearly naked children. Immediately, Orisha was embarrassed...and Pira felt sorry for Orisha.

Because it was Alice. One of the few women in all of Port Wolofu to actually own an automobile--and probably the only *unmarried* woman to be so privileaged. Even Pira, the mixed yellow wife of a lawyer (who provided television and internet telephone service in their home), could not afford to drive her own automobile. Obviously, Alice Maissa was a whore!

"Hi, big see-stuh!", sang Alice from her car. "And Pira-

-hello!" Alice giggled at the baskets atop their heads.

Pira smiled saying hello while Orisha murmured hers.

"Would you ladies like a ride home?", Alice asked her big sister. There was no shame whatsoever in Alice's face as people coming down the dirt road, especially Muslims, saw that it was a mere *girl* driving the car. She must be Black American, some of them thought, because she certainly looked like one. But most of the Christian grownups and children knew that she wasn't a wife, was barely twenty and was pure African harlot with a loud "O"!

"No", mumbled Orisha. "We make use of the walk home."

"Have you heard the exciting news?", grinned Alice.

"Exciting news?", sniffed Orisha.

"Yes. The cinema downtown--they're going to screen an Angela Bassett film next Friday."

A gasp of instant shock!

Both Pira and Orisha's eyes brightened and their hearts began beating wildly. "You're pulling one!"

"No, it's true. Women as far away as Accra are reserving the bus ride--and Mother Buchi Bala, the reverend's wife, she's having a dress made just for the occasion."

"Tickets will cost a fortune", worried Orisha.

"It's not often", mentioned Pira, "that we get to see an American film that features a black woman who actually *looks* African and makes us proud. It's usually that wonderful lion,

Denzel Washington, but more often, some insulting piece of trash like *Shaft In Africa* or Sidney Poitier playing one of his alienated grunting Pogo-nigger roles, but never the great Alfre Woodard, never the magnificent Cicely Tyson, never the soulful Halle Berry or Africa's own Thandie Newton. Never the beautiful and gracious Akosua Busia! Only in the magazines and from the mouths of rich women do we know about them. We *must* get tickets on reserve, Orisha! Immediately!"

"I already went to the theature", bragged Alice, Miss Sexy chocolate leopard whore! She raised three huge green cardboard tickets in the air and proclaimed, "I've gotten tickets already--for the three of us!"

Pira screamed!

Orisha and Pira screamed together! They jumped up and down, carefully getting firmer grips on their baskets. This was just the best news!

"I don't believe it", cried Orisha laughing, tears gushing down her cheeks. "We're going to see the Queen! Angela Bassett!"

~~

There is so much missing in West Africa these new days. That's what upward Pan-SeneGa women think about when they can afford to sit behind the glass of a window--like Orisha, Pira and Alice, comfortable in a cool livingroom like three dolls on Pira's lumpy green English tudor couch, pleasantly having warm tamarind juice and brined lobster rolled in tofu. For beyond the window, everything looks bathed in the white people's technicolor, the naturalness of life's journey taking on a fake smoke and mirrors effect. Even the pure African air that one breathes (so fresh and clean that visiting Black Americans swear up and down that it clears up their skin) seems foreign, manufactured and taxable.

"It's our damned government!", Tiju-Iku often hollers when he's drunk with his brothers, but only behind closed doors. "We need to have another coup. The president needs to be overthrown. Look at that rich baboon--black, fat, jolly Pogo-nigger bastard! He does nothing for the African people!"

Ring-a-ling. Ring, ring.

Orisha and Alice's middle sister, Akosua Nia, a student in London being educated, has telephoned Pira's home and says that her hair is thinning out, growing slowly now--from all the chemicals and European hair that she has weaved in her head.

"Then why do you do it!?", Orisha demands.

"Because in England, no black man will sing to me if I do not. Our natural African hair does not get his attention."

Akosua Nia does not mention to her sisters the cut lemons that she rubs on her chestnut-brown flesh, trying to lighten it, or the way that she has come to feel about her once sexy wide, flat nose. They would not understand how it is to be an *authentic* black woman--living outside of Africa.

She feels that the only African thing that is valued and

76

appreciated outside of Africa...is the tree branch between a black man's legs. To hell with his culture, his motherseed, his wooly crown, his natural mate, his dark giggling children, his self-respect, his timeless black dignity. He has become the world's most glamorous asswipe.

He, purely as himself, is considered more inferior than ever--and increasingly, by his own children.

Akosua Nia speaks none of this to her sisters. She plays happy as a roadrunner and shall return to them as a doctor of medicine. Good show, sister.

Truly, this is wonderful. The opportunities that the white man provides. Orisha, Alice and Pira drink a toast of palm wine and with each swig of wine, they pray good things for Akosua Nia.

There is no need for the window. For the sad black faces looking out...missing the vast, twisting beautiful jungles that were ripped up and hauled away from West Africa hundreds of years ago. And of the windows, too, they must be careful not to look too hard...for even the young begin to remember their mother's own negroid children that so-called Black Kings betrayed...sold away like cattle...they mustn't look out the window. If they do, then they begin to hear and understand what the very old African grandmothers are still screaming about! They begin to think that it is not just insane gibberish whenever they hear them say: "I have to get down to the beach! Let go of my arm! I have to get down to the water before grandmother drowns again!"

"No, you foolish old woman! That was just the sea!"

"Sea never dry", they sing with broken hearts. The shriveled up granddaughters of their mentally ill grandmothers. Wrapped up in all that crusty blue black skin and cottony white hair. Nobody paying attention to anything they say. Crazy old African muddcows! That's what the men call them.

But infinite is the sojourn. Peanut butter brown, eggshell tan, sweet luscious chocolate; Orisha, Pira and Alice stood together that afternoon. Prisoners of their flesh in ways that men will never be. Sisters. Looking out the window of love. In the tradition of African women, shedding more lonely light, more tears. So that in their uniquely haunted love; it becomes true...'sea never dry'. For in this shared state of all the black women in the world (and this is unique of the black ones), it makes no matter who you are or where you are, there awaits for thee, always; the leftover love.

tima, hoontabonbon, isjo...enchalla, amen.

~~

Tiju-Iku forbid Orisha to see the film starring Angela Bassett. He told Pira and Alice that she could not go. He said that Black American women were too contaminated by whites, too corrupt. "They hate a black man", charged Mr. Diop, to which a smart mouthed Alice had replied, "Well if they hate your black asses...then it's still not *half as much* as they should!"

"That's it! I want that whore out of my house now!"

"Alice, you have disrespected my husband for the last time."

"He's selfish, Isha! He choots on you every night! He doesn't appreciate anything you do for him...and now he forbids you to go and see Angela Bassett. I say to hell with all the husbands! It's time for a black girl revolution!"

Orisha slapped Alice across the face!--wifely proof of her devotion to Tiju-Iku, his manhood and his will. She said, "Now you get out of my husband's house, ungodly black leopard whore of Hedes!"

"The *black...MAN*", shouted Alice on her way out, "is the biggest disappointment since God!"

WHAM!

Bubble-butt pagan Alice slammed the front door as the seductive scent of cherrywood and wild lilacs tingled in Tiju-Iku's nostrils behind her. He got a slight hard-on.

"Alice is a whore. A traitor. She's just angry and I don't see why", Orisha struggled to explain. "But please, Iku--I want to see this film. It's *Angela Bassett!* We women have read so much about her and seen her photograph so many times. But her films, they simply aren't shown here. She and Alfre Woodard are the only African women who star in expensive, lavish American moving pictures!"

"Angela Bassett is no part African!", he shouted. "She's just another niggerbitch whore who hates men. Don't think for one minute that I've forgotten about *The Color Purple*--that disgusting piece of American pogo-shit!"

Orisha hung her head as he berated a film that was, for some unexplainable reason, very close to her heart. In fact, some women as far north as Nigeria and some others as far south as South Africa had raved so much about the film...that many African men protested against its exsistence and caused it to be yanked entirely from Pan-SeneGa theatures. It was then and still is now the opinion of most African men that any story told from the point of view of a *black* oppressed female--is a threat against male dignity and social respect for the clan.

"I want to see the Angela Bassett film", Orisha told him.

"There are other pictures playing", shrugged Tiju-Iku. "You can go see that other woman's film--the one starring..."

"I don't want to see that *white bitch!*", shouted Orisha. "I can see her anytime. She's in our face so bloody much, I can damned well see her in my dreams. *I want Angela Bassett!*"

"I forbid it, Orisha!"

Furiously, she ran to their bedroom. Tiju-Iku felt bad and followed after her. Truly, he did not enjoy arguing with his wife or making her angry. With whatever shortcomings Alice thought he had, Mr. Diop really did love Orisha...or atleast as much as he loved himself.

On the bedsheets, she weeped. He thought of a compromise and went to her. "Isha?"

She ignored him. So he said, "You may go to the film,

Orisha."

Surprised and happy, she looked up at him. she took his hand, singled out his middle finger and slid it inside the softness of her mouth. She sucked on it as he told her, "But only on one condition--you will straighten your hair for me."

Violently, she jerked his finger out of her mouth!

Iku's voice was stern, "This will be our trade off, Isha. It is the only deal I will accept. In exchange for soiling yourself by sitting through such a film that is against your husband--you must do something in return for your husband. I want your hair straightened."

~~

"STARRING ANGELA BASSETT"

Downtown Port Wolof was like a sea of rainbows, not a male in sight, as the hot afternoon sun reached down like nourishing hands cultivating a pungent wine--the women wearing flowing boubous of vermillion, crepe sepia, canary yellow, hunter green or tight fitting goddessa gowns of robin's egg blue and teal mercury; purple tye-dye geles or elaborate headpieces adorned with seashells or mother of pearl. Clergymen's wives, college educators, obedient housewives, government workers, fisherwomen and a few highly intelligent prostitutes all gathered as if responding to an urgent bell. They moved in straight lines; coming down avenues, getting off buses or being wheeled by the dozens in hand-pulled carts. Most of the government workers, nurses and prostitutes wore American clothes. Their hair was relaxed or hotcombed while the more traditional housewives, teachers and fisherwomen wore their hair natural with cowrie shells and handmade beads of copper, silver and gold. Those women without hair stole a page from the ancient Egyptians (who, both male and female, kept their heads shaven and covered with elaborate wigs) and donned synthetic black wigs with the little separated rugbells (denoting sexual athleticism) hanging off the ends just as the original negroid Egyptian queens had worn.

All around, it was a fashion show; a lively display of the women's personal style, and more religiously, it was the tradition of African women's inate glamor and creativity being showcased with all the historical pomp and circumstance of their foremothers--only much less epic and a tad less African.

Orisha, Alice and Pira PookBu were caught up in it.

Alice Maissa standing out like a sore thumb.

Everyone--absolutely *everyone* stared at her. Her blue eyes looked so real! Repulsive and ugly as it was, she really did look like a chocolate African with blue eyes, the likes of which hadn't been seen since old trader days when certain coastal children were the product of rape. But no half-castes had ever looked so deformed as Alice did now.

"Everyone is staring at you", Pira whispered nervously.

"It's because I'm so beautiful", Alice whispered back,

smiling arrogantly. "They think I'm a Black America diva girl, possibly related to Miss Angela Bassett even. I'm a star."

Alice then grinned broadly and tossed her flaxen black hair around, the blue eyes against chocolate skin projecting sheer terror throughout the crowd, because she looked like she was possessed by demons! Secretly, Alice was waiting for that one person, usually a man or a teenager, who would come up to her and say, "Why you look just like a pretty white woman."

Pira glanced over at Orisha and saw tears in her eyes.

Suddenly, several women who had noticed the marquee baring Angela Bassett's name alerted the other women to the big bold letters blazing overhead--and a wave of clapping rippled about. Applause, applause for an American movie actress who dared to *look* black, *look* African. A woman of class, dignity and great beauty. They applauded wildly!

Through it all, Orisha stood quietly.

Ashamed and speechless.

Her hair, much longer than she knew...lay atop her head...feeling as if it wasn't even there. Straight like a poisonous oil slick. So light that she felt bald. She could scarcely breathe without the smell of the chemical process whistling inside her lungs. Her heart itself seemed stepped on.

Inside her heart--it was all broken up. Not because Tiju Iku preferred her to look like someone other than herself, but because her own children had chirped compliments that morning. Telling how they liked it much better--this imposition upon her head made them appreciate what she looked like more, and with the realization that her children (her little chocolate angels) loved her more when she looked rather like Favor Lady than herself, it had forced Orisha, that morning, from her feet and into a chair. She waited til Yaro and Vashti were gone and then she wept and she knew that her heart would never beat the same again, because this is a betrayal before it feels normal.

The doorway into darkness opened now.

Orisha entered the theature with Alice and Pira. Completely hating, for the first time ever, half-white, stringy-headed Pira. In fact, she would never feel accepted or equal around Pira Pookbu again, she thought. How could Pira just stand by and let her be reduced and dehumanized this way? How could Pira, who claimed to be so African--how could she adore her own husband's African hair and yet fail to acknowledge, as biracial women do, Orisha's African beauty? Maybe Pira wasn't really black, but didn't want to be alone?

Thankfully, there in the darkness, finding a seat, people couldn't really see how strange and unnatural she looked. And it wouldn't occur to them that for some invading culture's ideal of physical beauty and acceptance...TijuIku had traded her in; sold her out. Already, some of her hair was falling out due to her not being used to the laboratory chemicals; the discomfort of what is not natural.

"I heard Angela Bassett is from Dakkar", someone whispered in the back row. "No-she's Yoruban!", another claimed.

"Her mother was born in Nigeria, but Un-julla got kidnapped as a baby and taken to America."

"Unjulla Bass-EET is from Na York, you fools!"

Speechless, Orisha sat back in the seat. Deep in the darkness. Perhaps Tiju-Iku was right--seeing herself Americanized on the big screen would only cloud her head with anger, disillusionment and make her begin to *think about* and *analyze* the world around her. See herself, for the first time, as *part* of the world instead of a servant (servant, African female, same thing) looking in. Wasn't that after all what happened to black females once they saw a beautiful and respectable towering image of themselves projected on a movie screen? Don't they begin to feel what white women have felt for a far longer time...that they are *part* of the *power* in the world? Even having a lot to do with shaping it?

In fact, they might even start to root for themselves!

They might start to *like* themselves (right at the cinema)!, and god forbid, they might even start to insist upon having a hand in how they are portrayed, projected and captured by the power of film.

Suddenly, the baby kicked.

One hand. Orisha's brown fingers. Reached up and touched the flat straightened hair.

Orisha Diop sat speechless. Truly feeling as though her tongue had been cut out of her head.

Time In a Bottle

I see her White. I see her Tan.
I decree what goes around; comes around.
I see her mutt fetus...slit open from the throat
to the anus and feasted on by rats.
I see every generation of those that touched her
...infected by an everlasting rupture; a
prevailing loneliness; a Psycho-misery of malignant
misunderstanding and cancerous disconnection.
I see her dreams dead beneath the ocean.
Everything she ever loved--shall crush her skull.

I see your fortune *falling*. Atu Imisi Kah.

She is but a tooth
rotting in the mouth of God.

I am God. I am the river of blood.

I set these powers of authentic love engulf
her
so that what goes around; comes around

From my country and my ancestors, I
set a promise cast:
Anu shaiba...kanu sijil...tima
Tima!

African Woman's Middle Passage:

White love's virus?/Chained Americus Black
Coal flung...fiddle one hell
abide another.
Folding back the covers of
the ocean's bed, O moon pearly night.
Folding back the whip-crackled blood
of Africa-man's impotent height.

In God We Trust, Miss Scarlett.
In God We Trust, Niggy...Wench (so indecently young).

Look to the fields...look how they grow.
Look to the rainbow, but you will not find her
authentic face.
Not in any history book. Or any Hollywood film *ever* made.
Nor any family photo album
on the negroid's clean coffee table.
In no one's recollected (intellect?)
For in sojourn, her children ripped her picture...*out.*
So black she reminded them of bondage absolute.
Fields die hard when you don't love them.

Folded back. In God We Trust, Niggy...Wench.

Of Americas of ships of silence *forever new* dwindling
baby's breath where white love's virus

compromised the brew.

And jellied blackberry juice drips a permanent
remark:
"See my hand?"

THE MAGIC WAND

Minx Nehesi:

*I am a healthy woman
of extraordinarily stunning beauty.
My life is blooming into an industry
of unlimited success.
I have an over-abundance of money.
I am rich.
Beyond my wildest dreams.
God is my help.
God is my love.
God is my shield.
God is my sword.
God rises me above mine
enemies
for his names' sake.*

*In Jesus name.
Amen.*

Sacred (The Magic Wand):

*Don't hate me because I'm a goddess...*or because I'm about to marry a white man or because I'm Ethiopia's hottest new super-model. Don't hate me. No woman is born to be hated, but to be understood--just like a man is born to be understood. Men and women, we are *both* born. And I am indeed Minx Nehesi, and yes, my mother was a bitch--but I'm a better one. I like my makeup...*even.* Oh! You think I have an attitude? Well just remember darling--*a woman is naked without one.* So pull up a chair and keep me company while they fix me up for the show. You can be my new girlfriend for the day.

You're a Black American girl? Saii-say?

Don't tell anyone, but sometimes I fantasize that I am a Black American. Yes, it's true! I have even mastered your accent to where I sometimes sneak around Black American women and pass myself off as one. I'm not snobbish. I forgive you Black Americans for being enslaved--and for never freeing yourselves from slavery but waiting on sympathetic whites to do it--and I like your style and how well you make your ego look like a gold medal. I think you are the prettiest women outside of Ethiopia, truly. Not that beauty is a virtue. It's not.

Here, eat this. It's from my country. *Enjera* (tasty bread). It's good, yoop? A-ha, baby sister! Take the slices of paper-thin beef there, take some sprinkles of cheese. Pour yourself the tamarind juice, baby sister. That's it. You have smoked fish and we can share this good yam with the melted butter. Come, baby sister. You and I have been at sojourn a long time and have not eaten together as we should have been all along. Eating together.

One time, I had an argument with a white co-model who accused me of having a "paranoid favoritism" towards Black American women. Can you imagine such dementia!? The idea that she of all plagues could legislate the heart and mind of so superior a being as an Ethiopian woman? *Saii-say!* Just between you and I, baby sister, I have to tell you that there is nothing more delusional walking the earth than these white whores. Truly, we must take pity on them...and play the game until they lose.

Well...don't get that look on your face!

Somebody has to lose. No wonder your people were slaves for so long! Everytime they touched your colored ass and said, "you're *it*, nigger!"...you went along with the program. Just accepted the life they gave you. As if you were inferior.

Anyway--I come from the city of Asmara. My father was the mayor and my grandfather served in the Dirgue, so you see, I started out with a great advantage. I admit it. I graduated university.

My mother was my father's wife. A beautiful woman. She stood colored the brave pagan yellow of Cleopatra, and as a consequence, I am blessed with the caramel-earthen-wine-dark flesh of Nefertiti. Kenyan cheekbones and all! Not that beauty is a virtue. It's not.

My parents call me "Kola". Because of the way I loved kolanuts when I was a child, it became my nickname. Oh, I do love kolanuts! Kolanuts and goat's milk with a little Egyptian sugar on my palm to lick off on a hot day! It really is special to be an African, baby sister. You should embrace yourself to be our blood relation. Well not that Black Americans come from Ethiopia, because clearly they do not...they come from the West African Kingdoms. But West Africa! The land of our mother's greatest warriors and genius art and your ancestors soul-dancing a fascinating rythm and beautiful midnight-black spirit women whose headdress and gown were more colors than we East Africans knew what to do with. West Africa. The bloodberry and the darkness. You must never let go of that. Saii-say? It is *that* which makes you beautiful, baby sister.

Don't tell me about your Indian blood, sister! After all, what praise can I give to a race that's nearly extinct? Extinction is not honorable! You see what passes for an Indian in America today and they're getting married to some white. What sense is that? None! So don't tell me about your Indian and Caucasoid blood relations, baby sister. It only reminds me of your enslavement, and when I look at your face, it is the part that reminds me of Ghana and Senegambia and Benin and Mali and Nigeria...this is what I respect and *cherish*. Not that you West Africans are related to us Ethiopians, ofcourse. Or even friends. But an African is still an African. We don't give a shit about the nigger blood you got from Indians and Whites.

Is that racist?

Good!

You Black Americans need to learn how to kiss your own ass sometimes. So you don't lose those pretty West African lips with all that syrup inside and that jawline and all that perfectly unique African hair, and especially, that gorgeous chocolate angel complexion.

Why then, you ask, am I marrying a white man?

Because I can never be *hurt* by a white man, that's why. I hate men, to be honest. They get in my way too much and I've always had a rule: find him, feel him, fuck him and forget him. It's a good motto for smart, financially independent women whose careers come first. But I guess I don't actually hate men. Honestly, I don't know. African women think I'm a whore, a traitor for mating with a white man, but I've often wanted to ask other black women, especially Black American women: "How do you continue to lay down with a man after you've lost all respect for him?"

Do I respect white men more than I respect black men?

Yes. I do. I definitely do.

Our African man is willing to sell his soul, to kill his own mother and poison his seed; our children--all for the sake of his inferiority complex. It's true. You don't understand how it is to be an African woman coming to America. Leaving a people to whom family means *everything*....in exchange for a nation where family means absolutely *nothing*. Please tell me.

What kind of Black *MAN* wants his son to look Arab or White? Sorry you don't like the word--*nigger*--but I think your people would be smarter if they kept the word and got rid of the niggers. They could start in the suburbs where the middle class blacks give that word its truest meaning. You don't think I have the right to say such things to you? Ofcourse I do, baby sister! I share the same birthright. Just as much right as these Whites you've been listening to and imitating for four hundred pathetic years! And that's too bad--what I said about our black man, but I don't understand this notion that I, the female, should be the one to hold his heritage intact and remain loyal to a selfish, self-hating anonymous black coward. I refuse to hurt.

You do it!

African men (and especially) Black American men--I don't owe them a goddamned thing. Not even a polite hello on the street. I care for them just like they care for me--*conveniently.*

If I could be a lesbian, I would, but the thought of it repulses me. Still, lesbians are the only women I've ever been jealous of. I really love Cheryl Dunye and K.D. lang and that Etheridge woman with all her camelshit. They carry a much lighter basket on top of their heads, I think. Man-free.

You think this is too much eye shadow? It looks like smoke.

I have excellent pussy. I keep my stomach muscles tightened and excersized at all times, and in America, it's good to have good pussy and a plan in your head. Heed on Minx, baby sister. See this extra-virgin olive oil? It was originally created for *our* skin. Just a little on our skin and on our scalp. Don't forget to eat green leaves everyday, whole grains, at least a yam a day to fight sickle cell, write letters to yourself, dance, drink water. Breathe correctly. Keep chemicals out of your hair--brush it, braid it, oil it. Surround yourself with people who are goodhearted and care about what happens to you. Whatever you really think--say it! Even if people hate you like they hate me. Honor yourself.

God, I have beautifully shaped lips. I always wear cranberry.

But yoop. Tis goot. Saii-say, baby sister?

You not feel like smiling back at me?

I have a gorgeous smile.

I finally told Leonard I will marry him. He could help me, you know. Him being a director and all. I might more easily make the transition from magazine covers to movie screens. I've always been a strong believer in self-improvement. And he's sweet. He's much older than me, but we have the most fascinating conversations. I think of him as a best friend, not a husband.

That's what I like about white men. They have a lot less stereotypes about us than black men do. And because we're not their own reflection, they can actually look at us and see how vulnerable we are. I have learned to cherish him. Ofcourse, Lenny's an exceptional pussyeater. O-twii, yoop. He licks this cinnamon swirl every dark majesty!

You're a christian, too? Like me? I was born Islamic, but Islam is not a religion for women, trust me. It's for pimps. Do you notice how the men made up all these religions to give us women plenty of rules and regulations--and then the men do whatever they want to do? They have a life and we have a man. That man usually being Jesus or Mohammed or some other ancient longhaired rock idol who can't fuck us.

To me, God is the energy of each human being united as one. God is the universe. But religion is the caveman's creation. Man's way of controlling different people and supressing certain impulses. I'm waiting for a woman to start a religion.

It's good, though. The Holy Bible. I read it when I need inspiration or when I miss my mother's sand-yellow face. So often.

Who is she? She *who?* OH! You mean the woman in this photograph taped to the mirror? The Jieng woman. I don't know her. She's a slave somewhere in Sudan. I keep her photograph because of the eyes--the power in her eyes. And that odd complexion. She's black as sapphire berries. But her Jieng eyes. I wish for mine to someday look that haunted against this Nefertiti-brown skin. Could you imagine!?

Oh, there it is. *Comiiing!*

They're ready for me to take the runway. I'm the most famous woman here tonight, so I get to model this stupid wedding gown. I'm keeping the bouquet, though. Sapphire berries and baby's breath.

(I lean down and gently kiss your forehead, baby sister.)

I know eeet. I'm a bitch. And while you Americans covet us Ethiopians--you don't *like* us. We are arrogant. Like your white masters, seemingly.

But always remember, baby sister...that those anonymous Africans who sold your ancestors into slavery...they're with you always. Yes, the ones who sold you.

Are in your beds.

They're on your court benches.

They're starring on your favorite black t.v. comedy.

They're straightening, perming and dyeing your hair.

They're rapping you a badass sweetback rap.

They expect your vote, your political support.

They're preaching to you from the pulpit.

They're rolling you a blunt.

They're judging you by what shade of black you are.

They're calling you *'sister'* and giving you the hand--to talk to.

So remember how much you love me.

I am not them.

I am you.

You.

From before you was you.

So that makes you and me us.

Like natural.

Black women. Baby sister.

I will always love you, because I love myself.

Now not a word of this to anyone.

Keep all my secrets--sacred.

I'm counting on you.

Beloved.

Black Beauty's Totem

I wish to find the swell
of constant waters

...and the death of the locust night

I wish to find the anguished heart
of the blue blackened earthquake
and lay my minkish head against his
armoured chest

to bless him with full, swollen lips
and behold his darkened portholes
drinking my softened flesh...oh, but yes

I wish to die as spirits then...

droplets

lost and swishing forever
deep within my purple folds
sweet

like birth and no regret

Nile River Bride
a True Story

You will hand-dig deep into the earth's moist blackness to find proper dirt. You smell it, feel it cold on your fingers, see it rich and black, red, gold, copper-wet. All that good dark soil that your *"ba"* can raise up out of. You need just to breathe.

In Sudan, the Nubians have a saying: "One handful of proper dirt is better than all the sand in the desert." So Caiphus Duany, who liked to rename things, could not think of a name for what he and his woman shared. He only knew that no such thing as a soulmate can be true, but *'kindred spirits'*--now that's true. For which there are many, making true love possible always. Anytime, anyplace.

"I found one", he often proclaimed while reaching his hand out in front of her smiling face, swooping up a fist of air, as though he'd snatched a butterfly out of flight. Overjoyed. *Kindred spirit.* "I found one!"

All in her breasts and throughout her heart (her book of magic), she felt warm and good about herself. As if they were haunted.

Like American jazz music. Which is haunted.

"You will be my woman?", he asked with authority.

To which she had nodded in agreement, shyly. The forest laced with all the sounds of all the centuries before them and orange sunrays cooling against their large foreheads as dusk was coming over the Nile swamp. She padded lightly behind him in agreement.

This was a good backwards place where there was no television to tell them who to love, no magazines imposing what they should look like, so they just looked and smelled like whatever the new day shined on--they breathed real freedom. Your curious heart (humanity's book of magic), spellbound, was like a dreamer irrational and relentless between them, casting quizzical glances and smelling for a familiar scent--studying for glimpses of personal style (originalities), likes and dislikes, sacred things...inside. Burried deep. Where the act of being actually matters. Inside...where you can *see* a person's insecurity and potential for survival or for good and evil.

Not civilization's love, but natural humble needful love--which to them was a hell of lot more civil.

Her father accepted Caiphus's pitiful dowry. His daughter was in love, and luckily, this was a father who cared more about his daughter's happiness than traditional bride-price acumen. He saw that she was actually turning womanwent. So at her wedding he placed African violets, very gently, behind one ear and wove with his own fingers the silk veil that covered her head, flowing beyond her shoulders. *Freely*...his daughter breathed.

Just like Kentake abu CanCollo Makeda (the Queen of Sheba), she was *very* black. Blue Black as sapphires unpolished. Sparkling and regal with Sheba's cutting cheekbones, the perilous eyes. All the wet liquid wonders of the ancient God of

Caiphus and his people--the crow. She was, on her wedding day, as black velvety and beautiful as the Queen of Sheba (Kentake abu CanCollo Makeda). *tima usrah. jazirah*...blessed motherseed; tima.

But she was not a queen. Nor he a king. They were up at the crack of dawn to chop down the sudd-cane jungle and to cut, shuck and stack far into the night. Their liquid black eyes dancing between them. Their lips red against the charcoal. Sudan like a great beast upon which they lived and sucked in life...and the Nile river; centuries behind them, and still, a crocodile too dangerous. Drumming. Beating in the background with the hands of the unseen. For Sudan's suffocation.

"I will have a son", Caiphus smiled.

She giggled. The more her belly grew. She giggled.

They ate. Freely breathing, deeply breathing, eating.

~~

Wedges of watermelon, fried locusts, tofu soup with yams.

Caiphus made a clearing under a tree where they dined before the long journey home each evening. By hand, his wife fed him.

Someone came to play music as they walked towards their village that night, the long road ahead of them. A small beige boy with that fine hair that looks like black silken spider silk. He tearfully played the lyresKerar--played it expertly. Telling tales of his own village being burned to the ground by the *murhaleen*--satan's Arabs in Africa; Egypt their protector!

Black African Christians disappeared everyday in Sudan. Slavery being their new occupation. *Slavery* on good proper dirt!

America's President Reagan, then President Bush, then President Clinton had all warned Islam's government in Sudan that they might do something about it. But they did nothing, not even breathe.

Anyway, Caiphus was determined that he and his wife would escape to Kenya or Ethiopia...if it went that bad. The beautiful lightskinned boy just played on. His music sweet as clear water.

Wife: *"im hunufiran saaqua palla mamluks-kaferi shiron"*.

Inside her, within the depths of his woman, Caiphus was very warm. And her overworked hands, the blisters on them, soothed. The two of them, their bodies, tangled in a timeless sleep. As all others, the beating of their hearts was our book of magic. Related to us. Unaware of the music or the cry of the damned. Collo-Jieng.

Their unborn child suckling the tiniest of thumbs.

Not hearing the soldiers coming through, wading through midnight's mysteries. *The footsteps.* Bringing coins for the beautiful boy, commission to keep his black jieng mother

103

safe from beatings and rape (or so they always promise such boys--rape babies). As we speak. On good proper dirt! As we speak, dearest father.

Those footsteps...beneath white whale moons of Sudan. *"I found one!"*

Breathing.

Remember, Son

Everything between us is the river and her bloodberry. I wanted you--because your father wanted you. At first.

Then...*I* wanted you.

Once my breasts swelled with milk and honey, I began to search for the right tree--I carved for you a greatly precise spear.

Ebony bark, lizard pelt. Good, sharp, jagged rhino's tusk.

As you are now, your head and shoulders between my knees as I braid God's masterpiece, this African hair--as my mommysweet once did mines. This, between Africans, is the circle of life.

"The burning bush", as Maphkela called it.

Ofcourse, it's not the way of African men to contemplate happiness.

We being natural people--it just comes for us. Easily as madness. Like song and dance. Like color and spirit. Truth, trust.

Love. Loyalty.

Everything we do. We do it as one, because that is the way of the river and her children. *That,* more than color, is blackness.

The river, the forest, the night and her music--there is no *individual.* No such thing has ever been. We are all--her results.

As a baby, you traced my cheekbones. Poked my eyes.

I knew that you would recognize the markings on my face, so deep and well-cut. But actually shaped in the name of all my secrets are these markings, and more than your father, you shall know my history. I will carry you on my back. You will know my songs. I wanted you, my son. I cried and ripped open to be your mother.

At that moment, I was a woman. Your father had spent weeks making one great drum after another. But the one that felt right to his palm and his heart, he gave it to me.

He said: "This one made the sound of our son's heartbeat."

That's how Maphkela men are, you know. People told him that I was ugly. But you will grow up and say that I was beautiful. On the inside. And that, for the first time, will be enough. They say that an ugly woman's son is the one to see her beauty. He is proud of her, because of her mothering. Proud and loyal to her forever after, they say. That's why I was so glad to have a son. Now I don't need beauty, because I have a son. An African son who loves me proudly.

Ofcourse, everyone will be gone then. Always, when you are African, people are missing from your life. To weaken you.

Your Papa cries like a child over how they dragged his mother away, when he was just starting to walk, to the witches' camp. Your grandfather's sister bore two stillborn sons in a row and accused Gnani of witchcraft, which in our land is all it takes, and the villagers beat her and stoned her and drove her to the camp where witches concentrate. Your papa never saw his mother again.

Others gone, too. Like my brothers, their wives and children all died from women's disease (AIDS). And our Chief and three of his wives and your father's father and his new wife. Even the most virtuous, saintly wives. Women's disease took them all away.

One brother of mines and two unlces, they died fighting with guns against the people who look exactly like us across the river, but aren't like us at all. My best friend from childtime, you remember her voice; *SallaraTongi*--she was driven away to the witches' camp for confessing that her brother raped her. They said that witches' blood inside her had caused her to seduce Kom, and because her father was so very blue-black, then his dead mother more than likely had been *evil*. Africans hate witches, and only women can be witches or create disease or be ugly. So people are missing from our lives.

Still, be proud my son. Your grandfather was a respected Witch Doctor and a mighty warrior. You have his flesh. Reddish-brown and wide of nose like a true river king. Boy magic.

Go away flies! Swatting them from your face, I tire not.

You are my King. Mother's spear, her drum and truest love.

I feel like a genuine person now, a true woman, because I have a son.

A son!

GNANI

Each dawn while picking cassava, SallaraTongi sings:

> *River Anyawu...issay taku*
> *Sweet Choco-lat*
> *Save it for you*
> *hope it will rain,*
> *hope I get food.*
> *River Anyawu...issay taku*
> *never my face, never been found*
> *meant to be a slave*
> *meant to look down*

Once a woman is banished to the concentration camps for witches, the river will never touch her or see her again. She does not exsist and is invisible. She has no people now. She is no longer loved. All she can do is pray to be found. By the river.

But she won't ever be washed again. Or human. Or anything at all, but a slave. For whenever she thinks of God, of the river--she looks down in shame; as she believes herself meant to do.

Own Me Night

She's the light reddish brown one, fetchingly plump with pretty eyes, who sits in the window cat-wishing, as though waiting to be painted. Just a little high on ganja. If two red birds skip across the pavement beneath her, she breaks into a smile so contagiously sunny that even God the infinite begins to giggle with her (deciding that no people anywhere can smile so beautifully as black people can).

Bhibo fell in love with her when she was laughing and her eyes were sparkling like the copper swirl in root beer candy. He had laughed, too, and said her name: "Nga'nsi. Be my river."

Youssou N'Dour was singing that afternoon. Something so tangible and wine-red dark that it made a stain across the room's silver-fished glow; pretty rain--and that's how they first kissed. Just as laughter is contagious, unexplainable sadness and need, they contagious, too! People begin to hold onto things that are natural.

Real close. Body to body. Dancing slow. Everwhere-you-could-want-to-be-close. Cat-wishing together.

"Your bed be sweet like honey", Bhibo told her.

"Long time before you'll find out", Nga'nsi teased.

See--that's mommysweet.

~~

Dance inside me, whispered her eyes another time. The night was all around them and calla lilies floated in a pond of lavender seahorses. His big chocolate snake wanted to get wet. So he struggled dancing, his hips trying to shake loose the discomfort.

Karaboo and Mogi arrived.

The two of them joining the dance magic, laughing with contagious orgy. And Nga'nsi and Karaboo were best friends and very hard on men, Bhibo thought. Their big smiling cheek-bones, so rank with laughter, seemed to lick at Bhibo's chocolate snake, and their scented flesh, the way they danced, it was like two silken salamanders together chanting:

Hooni-hoosi hole
Hooni-hoosi hole
Teasingly. Imitating babytalk. Say it:
Hooni-hoosi hole
Hooni-hoosi hole

Karaboo, who was the color of shiny-black jet-dark ebony with the whitest ivory teeth and a forehead so perfectly spooned that you knew she would give birth to a king--she asked if they would like to come back to her husband Mogi's flat? For drinks.

The men followed behind them. Watching the sway of their classic negroid bushwomen booty-nut. High, thick, cloved. *dukan* cake.

"I asked her to marry me", Bhibo told Mogi. "She said she has to finish university first."

111

"Drats!", spat Mogi. "Modern women!"

"Yes. The city makes them want to compete with men."

"I married Karaboo--she was seventeen and couldn't spell her own name. My mother came for a month and taught her how to cook my food. But look at her now--Nga'nsi arranged her that job cleaning up the library, and now she's reading books! She thinks she's a European woman. She wants to go to university and work outside my house--even after my son's born."

"What will you do?"

"I will knock her down when it's time."

"I miss the traditional mother-women", Bhibo said. "They knew how to be women. A man's foot was his foot."

"That's right, and they didn't dare cross over that foot."

"And speak of happiness! Our mothers were so happy!"

"It's America. America's ruining the whole world for us men."

Pussy.

An American word that the author of this book really appreciates, really loves, for reasons she doesn't fully understand. But hearing that word spoken soft and careful. It makes slush seem like ice cream, and implicit in a woman saying it--is power.

Whisper this poem softly:

Wet, sticky wine-dark sea. Choco/lat. Pink inside. Tight,

hot buttery muscadine. Sugar muscle/cinnamon swirl. Burnt bottomed black cherry-peach pooni. Soft and wet. Snicker-licker. Licka-dicka. Nandi pearl--coochy poon. Honey-tang, Egypto-julep bush. Muscle, muscle; *Cobbler.* Open peach meat...red...down the middle. Poon-tight-tumba-tang hooni boni. Brown naked, darkly wet Nefertiti...pagan yellow Cleopatra...sun golden Vashti...*Black* Sheba--Nalla--TinkaTekur--Iyanla--Hatsepshut--Kojinga--Sholoongo goddess Mumbi--Assis--Oshira--Iman--Olakun--Imani--Duniya--Ona *black pussy.* Black.

Man, woman and sin--African.

Hooni-hoosi hole.

For she is the sun.

Warm, wet finger. Whisper: *'starbright'.*

Bhibo was a filmmaker from Ogoni. It was his dream to follow in the footsteps of the most important black filmmaker the world has ever known, Senegal's legendary Ousmane Sembene. Bhibo wanted Nga'nsi to be his actress, because of her plump prettiness, but she fancied herself a psychiatrist one day--and that's what let Bhibo know that she was a natural born comedienne.

Oh what a laugh he'd get whenever she spoke of it.

"I'm one of the top girls in my class", she'd snap at him. A ball of fury in her chest as she realized that the male psychiatry students were allowed to study two years longer than the females for some unexplained reason. One of Nga'nsi's Professors had told her: "Too much psychiatry puts a strain on the female mind, it can even lead to hair loss and sterilization."

"Don't kiss me too deeply", Nga'nsi was saying now.

They were there on the couch, hugged up close while Karaboo put on some very mentally stimulating music by the great American genius, John Coltrane. Marvin Gaye, George Benson, and Nga'nsi's favorite, Erykuh Badu, would follow.

Karaboo danced a little. Tiny waist and thick spoon-butt.

"So when is the wedding?", Mogi teased them.

"As soon as I say it is", replied Bhibo, but Nga'nsi rolled her eyes, because she knew that he wanted to get her in bed so that she might become pregnant (downed like a plane). Mess up her education and rush a marriage. Still, there was no denying he loved her...as men love women. In their way, you know.

"I got fags", Karaboo sang as she glided over, three finely rolled ganja cigarettes in her hand. They loved getting high.

"Sit down flower", Mogi said and Karaboo sat on his lap.

Her dark black flesh, shiny with light, seemed to nearly transcend the see-through mesh of her silver-rainbow body gown, and her breasts and legs were so perfectly shaped that she seemed like a velvet painting. Lighting a faggot and breathing it deeply, snorting with a burning in her chest and then passing it on to Mogi.

Karaboo was a wife who really liked getting poked, and that scent of easygoing sensuality made Nga'nsi curious about it and lick her own frightened lips and stray from mere catwishing.

Bhibo and Nga'nsi lit their own faggot and sucked its fire.

"Dim the lights", Mogi told Karaboo. She got up and did as her man requested.

Bhibo took Nga'nsi's hand and put it on.

"Ouh dabawhi mafi toosi", moaned Karaboo with glistening black legs. "Oooh--shah!"

Nga'nsi pulled her hand back from Bhibo's lap and that damned Karaboo did more than dim the lights, she turned them off!

Dating in packs of four--this is done by Africans to *prevent* sex from taking place, not to encourage it!

And Karaboo, in the dark, made a strange sound: "sssss-ji-ouh!" *Oooh-shah!*

The hot center of Bhibo's large hand...it was over one breast, so hot and masculine that Nga'nsi felt like a small fetus again, and the thick wet sponge of black man's tongue was deep in her throat, too deep for sensibility or prayer, and she felt the tangy ghost-smoke in her lungs. "Oooooh-Sha!", she cried.

Wet slick for Bhibo's finger. Black God.

The river flooding to meet children's ashen feet.

Such a rich, fertile comforting darkness.

Black river man; Black God.

Sweetest father of time, sky and fire.

The river rising against the lungs of goats and children and black ashy mothers whose milk and honey hung heavy in long warm breasts. The drowning of breaths.

The poking started in the hallway.

Or atleast that's where Nga'nsi felt the first painful jab of ecstacy. Man's powerful tool of masculinity that pokes in us women like a root up through fertile earth. *Kasha!*

One of her legs seemed to be up in the air. Bouncing suspended over an arm of pure muscle. Bone inside her (granite?), relentless and hard as a thick unfeeling broom handle. In and out, in and out. You know how black men do that dance.

The fleshy wet big lips tracing her neck and jawline.

Dirt and water are what humans are made of.

Chocolate stick was all inside her humanity. Stirring the pink lava.

"Ouh-shi-domi! Ouh-shi-domi!", erupted Karaboo, suddenly screaming, like a mother giving birth.

A sweaty smack on the ass! Karaboo's bottom. Nga'nsi wondered if she'd ever be able to look Karaboo in the face again--them being in the same apartment while men took earth at the same time like this. Something this freaky, this kinky, this taboo...not even in films did decent Africans behave this way.

116

Bhibo's warrior-like muscularity suddenly seemed creased and cut.

But Erykuh Badu was singing so soft, so pretty. Brazilian basslines in the background. Lyrics lilting like honey. So pretty she sang-cried like some syrupy slave-virgin of jungle roundup days--the neck collar tight, the nipples hard and exposed, the pussy wet like tongues. Tied up and urinated on, awaiting master. Red knuckled beady-eyed white rooster.

Centuries go by and yet Spirit's body forgets nothing. Like the yesterdays when West African Pogo-Niggers (Uncle Toms in your dialect) would hold a young dark hairless virgin by the ankles, her legs wide open so that the chilly white fish-eyed (dead eyed) European men could inspect and appraise the pussy. And then the Pogo-Nigger would get his riches...handing us over by the back of our necks while clutching our wrists together tightly, explaining to the white men, countless times: "She different tribe--not my daughter. Here go good one, Paleface."

Nga'nsi opened her eyes suddenly. Her heart *stopping*.

She whimpered and began to cry, because it wasn't Bhibo inside her any longer. It was Mogi now! Mogi's nightmare penis.

She couldn't smell Bhibo anymore...and yet Karaboo had not stopped moaning and begging for mercy from the long thickness of the branches unearthing them. Karaboo was weeping. Crying out for help. Saying, "Make him stop! I belong to Mogi! Mogi save me!"

"No", protested Nga'sni audibly, but Mogi forced his hand over her mouth and kissed, nibbled at her ears and used all the force of his buttocks to reach inside her, to hurry up and have a finish.

"No!", Nga'nsi screamed out, tearfully. "Bhibo my master!", she cried out. "Only Bhibo!"

"Mogi my master!", shriek-cried Karaboo. "Only Mogi!"

Nga'nsi opened her eyes then. Falling out of clouds.

They were still at the club see. It had all been just a wet dream. Bhibo and Karaboo were out on the dance floor gyrating and twirling to the pimp-beat of American hip-hop. Nga'nsi had watched them with a tinge of jealousy, perhaps. Karaboo being so incredibly jet-black, shiny beautiful and Bhibo being so quietly displeased with Nga'nsi's personal ambition. And Mogi was engrossed in the Men Only conversations at the bar, his eyes red from all the cheap European Ale he'd consumed.

Just across the street--at the dance club for European tourists--African men were not allowed inside. Only African women, White women and European men.

Nga'nsi let her head fall back and tried not to feel so vulnerable in the world (that's what the word 'pussy' really means--*vulnerable*--and that's exactly what a vagina is--*vulnerable*), but at just that moment, she overheard some of the lyrics to the hip-hop song and realized that the word *'pimp'* was in every place that the word *'father'* should be and that the words *'bitch'* and *'ho'* translated into 'mother, sister, daughter--female'. Do the Americans, she wondered, realize that what continously comes out of ones mouth and goes into a younger one's ears is what will eventually come to pass?

For in all man's creation, there is not a bomb, a vaccine or a bullet that can compete with the power and the infinity of *words*. Words can create and words can *kill*.

If it is recited, if it is written--then it will be.

So that when Bhibo came off from dancing and walked up to Nga'nsi...she pulled him close to her and told him in his ear, "I love you, blackman. Forever. I yours, you mines. We responsible for this land, for all Africa, because our graves are just the same. I love you black man...like you growing inside me."

Bhibo delicately enclosed her left ear between his two rows of straight bone-white teeth, clenching the lobe, and dreamt her pregnant like African men like us.

ARROGANCE

Ten lions surrounded the tomb at dusk and twelve concubines could be glimpsed at dawn, married to the lake--the scarlet wine of their young veins like a red dye cast against lavender white-stone water; the bloated white ashen mouths that were dark with the longing for his kiss. So as now burned a fire, a great pillar of stone in Timbuktu. King Muhongo, the living God of Timbuktu, was dead in the sun and asleep to all wishes. Conquerors had removed first, his penis, and then his head--and had stolen his tongue, his eyeballs and cut off his hands. So that on her knees, Queen Doja was nothing now but the dark ash of the women from the earth's core.

Throats tightened as she took her stool.

The divine and bloody goddess of Timbuktu--*Queen Doja!* (Red eyeballs instead of white).

The scarification welts--*faith* slit inside the cheekbones.

"Greetings little child."

"You betrayed my husband", replied the Queen, weakly.

"Your husband would not receive Allah--the God of all mankind, little child. Allah is God."

"I have buried *God!* I will give birth to him again."

"But no, Doja. You will marry Allah. You will be covered up, protected, held high in love as a symbol for your people. And they will rejoice in Allah and be saved from the lava. Never

120

again will you stand with your breasts bare and your scent so loud or your legs so naked. Your black face will have Mohammed's light upon it and you will become a woman.

"But I am more than a woman. I am the divine and bloody goddess of Timbuktu--I am Doja! Black panther of the mountain cave and red river of creation. I am not naked, but infinitely divine!"

"You shall marry Allah or die!"

These conquerors, these dark chocolate foreigners with the strangest stick-straight hair, they drew their swords and skullcrushers and licked their pink lips as though thirsting for Queen Doja's raven black liquid flesh.

"Then you choose damnation, little child?"

"You haven't a heaven or a hell that you can put me in! You're nothing but a man! A beast that comes out of my ass at best! I am Doja! Black panther and red river of time. I am purity and all that is true. I am a witness to the earth, the wind and the fire. I am dirt and water. I am *rain*! I have burried God and will give birth to him again. My father lived beneath the lake and my mother tended the trees of the forests! I am a dolphin, a lion, a black panther! I am Doja. Divine and bloody goddess of Timbuktu."

"Kill her...in the name of Allah!"

"Arrogant fools!"

Sw-iick!!

and roll...lightly bouncing; roll.

Atop the Holy Koran, they lay her bloody head.

Day of Vow

She stuck with it...being a glassmaker. When you make glass, there's an experience as it forms when the matter is so fiery liquid and lava-taffy hot, becoming more and more of itself like the ocean that it is literally intoxicating and otherworldly hypnotic. Like something from Mars or hell or inside the sun. Beautiful as anything you could dream about paralyzed. That's how it felt having the privileage and the blessed luck to make glass for a living.

It wasn't a normal job for a South African woman, educated or otherwise to occupy...but Zorina had been doing it since she was eight (the house maid's curious little daughter back then), and now at seventeen, no one at the furnace could match her craftsmanship. The Theron family was making quite a name (not to mention a pretty penny) for itself because of this quaint little wonder, and Zorina, too, had an obsessive interest in their manorborn. Miss Lindy and sweet little Cribbitch could absolutely send one.

But the person who really intrigued her, even more than glass, was the Theron family son--nineteen year old polo champion Noble Theron--who had raped Zorina when she was thirteen. The Theron's called him "Golf". He was tall and handsome, chilly white with an innocent soldier boy's face and warm glacier-blue eyes. He fascinated Zorina to no end, mainly because he had lived for a while in what she considered to be life's promised land--America; and then, too, because he had raped her and then seemingly forgotten all about it (as if she had just imagined the whole thing)--and this only increased Zorina's pain until all she could do was pass out from it (have a nervous breakdown) or become fascinated by the source of that pain.

"Haven't I told you not to call me Golf when we're alone, Zora?"

"Yes, Noble", she always replied with as feminine an incantation as possible.

At the mere sight of him, Zorina always felt dizzy in the tummy and weak in the knees. Like most white men in South Africa, Golf moved about like a stern wire coathanger.

"And do sit down, girl. I want your delightful company more than any breakfast. You know that."

On the veranda's cool dawn, the sun barely up and cloud white butterflies fluttering about the garden, Golf Theron took his milk with a spoonful of cognac and his oatmeal with cream and sugar. They sat together; two extremely secretive people. Zorina more than him--because only she knew about the little match box that she kept in her skirt's front pocket and the tiny black pellets inside (rat turds). Only she knew how metallic and perfectly formed they looked, like little black rice pods, as she took a few out each morning and stirred them into his oatmeal right after her mother cooked it up. And every morning, for years, he had eaten it all down, and that's what helped Zorina justify her love for him. She thought that he must be as poisoned and tricked inside as she was by now. Her being raped at Theron Estate and violently burned at school and his stomach full of rat turds made them seem perfect for each other.

"So you've heard about the tennis match?", he asked Zorina.

Her face, a lemony ice-tea color, was instantly lit with a grin. Like all the other South African black girls, she had cheered the arrival of Venus and Serena Williams (Americans!) and had been overjoyed to see an African-*looking* girl play tennis and beat the turd out of Amanda Coetzer, South Africa's white champ. All over the country, in the streets and- dirt roads, the blacks had cheered and rooted: "Go Venus!, Go Venus!" As if *Venus* was the South African. So yes, Zorina had heard. Her mother had even made a keg of beer for the ghetto's celebration and black fathers had danced barechested in the streets with *VENUS* written across their hearts in the bloodiest red paint they could find.

Golf Theron blushed and gave a cave-dark grin. He whispered across the table, "I was rooting for Venus, too."

Heat covered Zorina's forehead. Like it did every morning when Golf was done with breakfast. Because that's when he always rose, towering over her...and swaggered on by, deliberately brushing his athletic hairy leg against her lean brown arm. For a split second, she remembered his weapon of authority; erect--the only manpart she had ever known. His

124

mighty white skin touched her clean brown embarrassment. His white tennis shorts, the ones that Zorina's mother washed and ironed in stacks each week, seemed so fresh and pure; so sunshine bright and snow white.

Whiter even--than the sickle shaped burn seared into Zorina's right buttock like a pothole of saintly white ashes.

"Carry on, Zora."

In a breathy voice.

"Yes...Noble."

But once he was gone and her mother had cleared away the dishes he left behind, Zorina always managed to turn back into herself. Humming some American pop song (*"I Can't Tell You Why"* by the Eagles) as she left the veranda and passed Miss Lindy's gazebo, the swing set for Cribbitch, the heavenly green arc of field and forest that shaded the horse stables...and finally, on down the dirt road past the creek, her favorite place in the whole world...the Theron furnace.

Three brick chimneys pointed up from the old building like a crown and the trees on either side of it seemed ageless and ancient--brittle gray and undying. Zorina's mother always told her that "trees are loyal beings". The furnace house was made of granite with a cobblestone floor inside the entrance hall. On the hook outside, she always hung her sweater before placing a sak lunch in the little locker that made her feel accomplished and important, because it had her name written across it in typed ink. Golf Theron had done that.

Ebaneezer called out, "That you, Milady!?"

"Yes it is!", Zorina hollared back with a grin.

He was having breakfast in the nook. His face pink like strawberry ice cream and his chin and cheeks always foaming with a white unkempt beard. He was a fat, stinking soot-covered Santa Klaus-looking man with ale on his breath and gas passing from his arse every twenty minutes...but he had a heart of gold.

Zorina entered the nook. "Balu inside already?"

Ebaneezer nodded and farted.

Balu was the new glassmaker from Cape Town. He was Indian and had a wife who was half-black, half-Korean...and since the two of them were legally coloured (which is a *higher class* than plain old black in South Africa), they didn't allow their two children to play with black, kinky-headed kaffir kids. Balu had told this information to Golf Theron (to affirm, as coloured South Africans do, his loyalty to whiter sensibilities) and then Golf had turned into Noble and told Zorina. So Zorina didn't like Balu--because she knew a lot of Indians, Asians and mixed race people that were like that. In fact, according to her dead father, Africa was infested with them.

The other glassmaker on the premises, Othello, he was mixed-race, but he wasn't like that at all. For whenever whites called a black person "kaffir"--it was as if they had called Othello himself that horrible word. He considered himself an African and would say it out loud to anybody's face. His wife, however, was as ugly as raw liver according to Zorina's mother. He could've had his pick instead of choosing a girl who was so darkskinned and walked and talked with the smell of sex in her personality. Him being such an eggcreme pretty fellow with a good job and so ruggedly mannish with those big soccer legs and that curly Italic hair (his father was Italian-Lebanese and his mother was a black South African woman, herself part Indian). Wasting himself on some low class chocolate kaffir bitch, Zorina's mother would say. Here he was now.

"Greetings, Zorina!"

"Hey...top of the morning, Othello! How's LissaMondi?"

"Oh, mighty good going. The baby kicked this morning and Lissa graduates from nursing school next saturday. I'm inviting everyone for stew and bread. You bring your Brenda Fassie albums, Zorina!"

"I'll have to sneak them past Big Mama", she laughed.

The flames resemble pieces of hellfire tumbling around like clothes in a washing machine. Capable of baking the face six shades if one doesn't wear a protective mask. It's hot like an oven down there. The sweating is unavoidable and yet the skin beneath the sweat remains dry, parched and crackly. The blistered smell of the liquid glass as it's looped and spun, twirled or blown...transformed from recipe to imagination to creation's beauty both challenges and resists Zorina everytime, but her standard of taste is not a will bestilled.

"Hers are special", Balu whispered enviously whenever she set a sea-crystal wine goblet atop the cooling board.

"She's gifted", snorted Ebaneezer, as if Balu had better recognize that he is not the big maestro he thought he was back in Cape Town. He's just a talented backup singer now.

"Damn, that's pretty", said Othello as he glanced at the intricate spheres, the way the light was alive beneath the precise layers of Zorina's spooling sheath. He got a lump in his throat just looking at it. Her creations looked more like jewelry than tablewear.

"It's all in the wrist", bragged the little brown girl.

"No, no...the heart", smiled Othello, tenderly.

~~~~

In the late evening when Zorina and her mother took the state worker's bus from the back road of the Theron Estate all the way to the dirt roads of the ghetto shanties of Sowego, the transition felt as normal to them as breathing. They were slightly higher class than most of their neighbors, because being the head maid for a family as rich and well known as Dutch Theron's was a major coup, and more than that, Zorina's status as glassmaker provided her the rank of a college graduate and surpassed all the menial factory jobs that the local men were allowed to hold. She and her mother were looked up to.

"I need time for the wedding dress", sighed Etah, Zorina's mother, as the two of them busied themselves setting supper in the small of their kitchen. "The hours inside the night just aren't deep enough."

Zorina, solemn and deeply breathing, tried not to burst into tears.

Etah was a hefty woman with a profound pair of buttocks and huge feet like a camel's. In the center of her face she was pretty. She greatly resembled the beautiful American actress Alfre Woodard, her spitting image, only Etah was fat and had much lighter skin. She wore a rag around her head and sometimes grimaced from the arthritis plaguing her knees and left shoulder. Her man had been dead for years, so her thinking skills weren't as whiplash quick as they had once been. Mainly, she let herself settle into acting a lot older than she actually was and looking like, too.

"Oh...I've got to sit down."

"Big Mama, get off your feet now."

Zorina had the pot of red beans, rice and oxtails heating up (leftovers), and Etah would just have to make herself a little pan of peppercorn broth to go over the bread. Her late husband had always loved having his peppercorn broth over some bread.

"I've got to work some with that dress", restated Etah, and Zorina's heart jumped again at the mention of it. She could just imagine all the lavish white lace, satin, tulle...flowing beneath the soft pretty whiteness of Maritza Buitengracht--the proper young lady who was engaged to marry Golf Theron in just another month.

"Let her buy a dress in Durban, Mama. They'll shop and horse race this coming weekend as it is."

"Miss Lindy wants Maritza to wear the same dress that she wore. It needs lots of alterations, because that Maritza girl is no bigger than a strand of straw. Skinnier than you, Zorina, if that's possible."

"You think Golf really loves her, Mama?"

"I think he's like any other man entering marriage--he'll act out what he's seen others do. But it's Miss Lindy that picked her. Brought her back from Europe and set it up. She sure is a lovely girl, I'll say. Just as beautiful as a snow white princess from a land of angels."

Instantly, Zorina recalled the time that she and a friend had been in line at the cinema house and overheard a group of handsome black boys repeating a saying that's very popular among South African black men. Two boys told another boy: "White women don't need to take baths, because God made them clean by nature and they never smell."

Zorina blacked out just thinking about Maritza's long, golden tresses of angel's hair and the gorgeous way it flowed heavily down her back like wavy yellow sunshine. She floated away thinking about how Golf always held that dainty little white hand and kissed it just so...like it belonged to a Queen.

"I hate Golf Theron", Zorina heard herself say. Her voice tight and mean. It surprised and startled Etah.

"But what, my daughter?"

"I said I hate Golf Theron, mama. He doesn't deserve a beautiful white woman like Maritza Buitengracht, she's too good for him, mama."

Etah rallied back with her maid-like instincts. She insisted, "But Golf has *always* been a good boy! He's as handsome and kindhearted as a man could come, Zorina!"

Zorina almost mouthed off and reminded her mother of the time that Golf had told classmates visiting from his boarding school that Etah was part of an ancient ape tribe and then asked her, right in front of all those white giggling faces, to speak "planet of the apes language". But Zorina said nothing.

Teardrops, huge and wet began swelling and falling into an emotional breakdown as Zorina screamed out, "If I could rip out his throat, I'd do it! With my bare hands, I'd do it!"

"*What!?*"

Etah was no dummy. She'd seen that kind of bitterness in the eyes of black worker-bee women before, but she couldn't risk hearing what might come out of her daughter's mouth next. For if it came out to be rape, then Etah might have to do something about it, and courage had never been Etah's strongsuit. So instead, she jumped to her feet and slapped the living shit out of her daughter!

"*SHUT...UP!*"

The shock of it stunned Zorina to complete stillness, her eyes bulging and her back tense as though a pan of cold water had been dumped over her head. "Now you stop this jealousy you have towards white girls and thank our sweet lord for the privileages that you do have, you selfish black arse! I won't have you say another bad word against Mister Theron. He's a good boy, educated and handsome and he treats you like you're his own sister, Zorina! You don't know how spoiled you are by the Therons, that's the problem! He lets you call him *Noble*, and not even his own mother calls him that! What's that? You thought I didn't know your little secret?"

An iceburgh moved between them.

"Alright then, mama", whispered Zorina. "I...*love* Noble."

Then she left her supper on the table and went up to bed.

In the dim light of her bedroom, fully unaffected by the sound of mice playing in the walls, Zorina stood naked in the half mirror staring at herself. She couldn't imagine how anyone could think for a single moment that Maritza Buitengracht was more beautiful than she was. Obviously, Noble knew the truth. He was the one who always insisted that Zorina looked exactly like the gorgeous movie actress Thandie Newton (only Zorina was four shades browner)...and wasn't it *Zorina's hair* that had fascinated Noble when she was just a child? Hadn't he marveled at how soft it was--natural, springy African hair worn in a medium afro? Hadn't Golf liked putting his hands in it often (without permission as white people do)?

From Golf, Zorina had learned that nothing gets dirty faster than *white* skin. Or can smell more foul. So black men in South Africa certainly didn't know what they were talking about.

Carefully, just as she did every night, she applied several coats of pure vitamin E oil to the burn on her bottom.

Zorina thought this whole entire world must be insane to think that Golf could find a better woman than her. But then again, white men were different from other men Zorina had observed. White men admired themselves and their race far too much not to give birth to purely white children. That was the catch, Zorina realized. It was their own white children that they loved so dearly, more than life itself, and for that, she couldn't help but respect them.

Zorina pulled the covers over her head and drifted off to sleep.

Once asleep, she was back at Children of Christ Protectorate School. Eve was holding her hand. She could see the charred black door again...lava red beneath the blackened wood. The only classroom was burnt down around it, smoke everywhere. Most of the children beneath the rubble were burnt to a white crisp. It was a black school (without whites or coloureds), so the fire brigade didn't arrive until the next day. But Zorina had escaped with her life.

She had lived to see the newspaper headlines that blamed the fire on radical white men protesting Mandela's *new*

South Africa, and within hours, the entire world was outraged to learn that white men had burned up forty-two innocent little black children. Riots broke out...for three days straight.

Riots.

But Zorina and Eve looked at each other now.

They knew that it wasn't white men who had deliberately burned those children to death, the teachers, too.

Etah laid in bed like a whale and cried like a baby. Above her head hung the portrait of Queen Elizabeth II that her husband had proudly nailed to the wall on the very first day that they had moved into the house. In fact, after carrying Etah over the threshold, the portrait had been the first item of decoration that he'd carried into the house, even before a single piece of furniture. His mother had cherished it all her life and given it to the young couple as a life's luck gift. She bid her son to respect it as if it were she herself. So Nopopie had adored the portrait of Queen Elizabeth II, and now by laying beneath it at night, Etah felt that she was especially close to her late husband's spirit. She believed that through Elizabeth II, Nopopie could hear her more clearly.

"Nopopie...it is me, again. *Etah*", she cried. "I feel as if none of our children have understood the warning in your murder, dear husband. The way those white devils kicked holes in your stomach and left you in the church restroom to die. Like you were just trash, dear husband."

The police had claimed Nopopie assaulted one of them after they had politely asked to see his traveling permit.

"I worry about Zorina", she weiled, tearfully. "I fear she's been compromised, like your mother and sister were when you were just a boy and couldn't protect them."

His smell came into the room, because Etah missed him.

She missed the way he said grace at mealtime.

She missed the times when he drank and cursed the white overseers who worked him mercilously at the mines, making him beg every week for that pitifully low paying job, and then talked down to him like he was a boy.

She missed the times, right after Nopopie had brutally beaten her (clocked her upside the head with his boot)...the times afterward when he would pull her long, wide skirt up over her head and plunge his manhood deep inside her. She ached for the banging and the wretched sobbing—of a man sincerely sorry about the cruel ways inwhich he abused and humiliated her.

"I love you, my Etah!"

"I know you do, Nopopie. I know you do", she used to cry, so patiently, as her eyes were swollen shut and blood ran from her nose and busted lip.

Other times, he would beat her up and then take out his manhood and urinate right in her face. All in her hair and down her pregnant belly. "I can't afford all these kids, bitch!"

But she missed him now so much that she'd gladly go through it all again. Every moment of hurt and humiliation.

135

Just to see him, touch him and know again...that he loved her.

Etah got up and put on some music. Miriam Makeba, Etta James, Burning Spear. She took her headrag off and greased the thick, soft African bushhead. Hot tea was sipped down. Prayers to Jesus Christ were hummed, spoken and cried passionately. She promised herself that she would clean up Miss Lindy's massage room real good tomorrow and get that blasted dress worked on.

Then she slept...and snored tremendously.

Eve's Monkey had been missing ever since the fire.

Zorina bolted upright in bed!

Awake.

Breathing hard.

Wondering if it were Eve and Jesus Christ again--outside her window, standing barefoot on the dirt road--calling her.

She wished it were...but it wasn't.

She wished Winnie Mandela was her mother, but she wasn't.

She wished everyone knew that Golf Theron just couldn't get her out of his mind, but she was a kaffir girl, and therefore, no one would *ever* believe it.

She wished her classmates hadn't screamed so horribly as their flesh burned, their bones crackled like firewood and their lungs strained, coughing.

She could still hear them.

She could still hear every last one of them.
Crying out wretchedly for their mama's.

~~

Before dawn, Zorina and her mother were back at the Theron Estate. Preparing the house for when everyone awakened. At daybreak, Golf arose to have his usual oatmeal with his usual rat turds while Zorina sat by waiting to be brushed up against before a long, satisfying tournament of glassmaking.

It had been nine years since the school burned down, but as Zorina was experiencing cramps that morning and the start of her monthly bleeding, it didn't seem so long ago, because along with her monthlies always came a nagging pain in the scar tissue of her burn. As though the burn were new again.

"What's in that pretty little head, ha?", asked Golf. "Keeping secrets are we?"

"No...Noble."

In the beautiful oceans of his blue eyes she thought that she wanted to backstroke naked. Feel the beating of his heart against her warm golden body. Be swept away.

Suddenly, Etah appeared--filling up the back door in her giant maid's uniform. She had none of Hattie McDaniel's famous sass. No subdued outrage like the American star had shown in all her gallant portrayals of black maid women. Etah was a *real* servant spirit. "My daughter?"

"Oh!....ahhh...yes, mama!?"

"Miss Lindy would like to see you in the library."

"Is that my Zorina!?"

"Top of the morning, Miss Lindy."

"You've got to get packed dear. We're flying to Durban."

"...ew...wu...*Durban*?"

Cribbitch, her sweet blonde crystal-blue eyed little daughter chimed in with: "Mummy's having a glass show at the Wedgwood Gallery."

"Your glassworks are making me famous, Zorina!"

"But, I haven't anything to wear."

"It's alright, love. No one expects a black to be dressed that well, but I want you to represent the furnace workers."

Miss Lindy, who lead people to believe that she actually designed and self-crafted the Dutch Theron Glass Collection, hadn't been inside the ahouse for twelve years. Her husband, Dutch, had a reputation for taking his Indian whores down there at night, so Miss Lindy refused to set her wifely heels on those sticky floors.

"Oh, Zorina! They're giving me an *award!*"

"Glassmaker of the year", chirped Cribbitch.

It never occured to any of them (not even Zorina) that the award should be given to Zorina.

"Hurry home and pack", cheered Cribbitch. "We've already told Etah that you're going away."

~~

Zorina tried to remember how the poem went. *I come from a place...*

As the plane lifted out of Johannesburgh and creased blue sky towards Durban, Zorina tried to remember how the poem went:

I come from a place...but my place is not named for me
I am the caretaker, unnamed,
the insider
whose heartbeat your hear.
I have no place...not even my own
footprints
have any place.

She had never seen how breathtakingly beautiful South Africa is from the sky. How earthen brown and green and soulful the landscape is. An African's dream; kissed by God.

"*My place*" Zorina thought...as tears ran down her dark cheek and she thought of her devoted mother, her dead father. *Mines!*

One day, she prayed, all the whites would be gone from South Africa. So that the black people could take the time necessary to get over all the cruel and inhumane evils that the Europeans had so lavishly carried out. Even in the name of God, they had carried out unspeakable evils that could never *really* be forgtten. It seemed so unfair, their being here...living high and mighty off the backs and the land of Africa's true

139

children.

Zorina wondered how it felt to die by having community police kick holes in your stomach? And knowing how many black men and black women had experienced such horrifying deaths in South Africa, she wondered how many *whites* had experienced such evil?

"Remove them, God."

Zorina put her head back and stared out the window to the gliding wing of the plane (she was seated alone). That's when Eve's face popped into her memory. Little girl Eve. So charcoal black that she wasn't allowed to be registered at Children of Christ Protectorate School...even though it was founded, funded and ran by two black men. Eve's charcoal coloring prevented her from attending, and two decades before that, Eve's mother, one of several dozen *charcoal* prostitutes, had been deterred from seeking education due to the same skin problem.

The secret came back to Zorina now.

"It's morning time!", one of the black Reverends had said when Eve's Monkey tried to register.

These two Bantu clergymen, schoolteachers, were of South Africa's popular belief that the black race was moving away from oppression and the *darkness* that caused that oppression. Girls like Eve were a threat, because no one wanted those genes passed on.

Little charcoal black *"boys"* (in fact, one of them was Eve's very own brother) were allowed to attend classes. But whenever a charcoal black girl tried to register--the men did not allow it. Why even the two girls as chocolate as mudd were allowed in--but not girls as charcoal black as Eve's Monkey.

"Don't call me Eve's Monkey!", the seven year old barefoot girl had hissed back at one of the clergymen one day. "That's not my name!", the girl had cried.

"Well, you look like a monkey!", retorted the Reverend. A grown man, a chocolate-skinned man, a man of the cloth. "And you won't be enrolled here, you smelly, ugly little oil stain! It's morning time!"

Everyday, Zorina had witnessed it. The little blue black girl marching barefoot, dressed in rags to the school building. All the other girls her color had accepted their rejection on notice, but not this nervy little black thing. She was brave!

"I want to learn to read and count my fingers!", Eve's Monkey would beg.

"Go to monkey and ape school, little prostitute!"

Brilliant laughter.

Zorina could see all the children now. Little chocolates, milky browns, golden browns, light browns, yellows, *blue black* *"boys"*--and especially Sowego's majority color (peanut butter browns)...oh they had a belly laugh! Little girls with Afros, pigtails and some with long, thick black perms--they shot their shining brown eyes at Eve with venomous disgust.

141

"You're too ignorant to learn!', shouted Eve's own brother. "You're so ugly, the school books won't stay in your hands!"

"They left you in the oven too long!", shouted one fat yam yellow girl.

"Why doesn't she grow some hair!?"

Zorina could feel it again now...*the heat* and the pain and how everyone was suddenly in flames and the roof caved in and lucky for Zorina, she was away from her desk sharpening her pencil by the only door that led outside. She had braced her nose against the gasoline fumes as she ran out...and she had spotted Eve running through the green pastures barefoot, dressed in rags, laughing.

She had watched Eve running, in fact, until Eve evaporated into the hillside...like a ghost. Then other dead children, children whose bodies were still burning inside the school, they began following Eve into the hillside...as if they were all going away to play together...and that was when Zorina fell in love with the fires that shape glass. Their spirits had all looked like clear glass objects to Zorina, joyfully leaping into a careless paradise. Zorina had wanted to go! Everyone else was going! But one of the dead boys yelled, "You stay here!"

Zorina was just eight then...and no one thought to put her into therapy for what she had experienced, and ofcourse, the tragedy would be blamed on white men's racism, not black men's racism, but Zorina couldn't have cared less if white men were held responsible for it.

The hotel in Durban was exquisite. Unfortunately, Zorina's traveling with Miss Lindy and Cribbitch always meant that she would act as surrogate maid and secretary. She had to unpack and hang up their clothes properly, prepare their baths and fix their meals, because Miss Lindy always reserved a suite with its own well stocked kitchen. She couldn't even tell them that she was bleeding. That's how genuinely close they were.

Meanwhile, down the street, cases of the glass pieces, almost every one of them conceived and crafted on the spot by Zorina, were pulled out of padded boxes by specially trained handlers and aligned along the gallery walls. Lindy Theron was there to marvel at the wonders that bore her husband's good name. She couldn't wait for the awards presentation dinner!

"We should get a dress, mummy", said Cribbitch suddenly. "A dress for Zorina to wear. It's her big night, too. She hasn't anything to wear and she's so pretty, mum."

"I guess I could do that much", nodded Lindy. "I don't want her standing behind me in the photographs looking like some unfed praire dog."

Back at the hotel, Zorina sat suddenly on one of the beds she was custom making. She was dizzy and bleeding and felt like she was dying. Her cramps were like stomach punches!

She lay down on the bed...flat...and stared up at the ceiling.

Out of nowhere, she began to miss her mother, intensely, as if she might not ever see the plump, pretty face again. Zorina had always been a girl who knew instinctively that *mothers need their daughters*.

And she loved Etah more than anyone in this world.

"O...", gasped Cribbitch. "That is so pretty on you!"

Zorina couldn't believe she was being fitted in such a gown as the one Cribbitch had picked for her. Cribbitch might only be twelve, but she was a very sophisticated little girl and her taste in clothes was impeccable.

Shiny, lemon-tea light brown with the loveliest face and a perfect crown of cottony African bush hair on her head, Zorina looked like a Zulu princess in a strapless, flowing white Athenian tube gown complete with golden arm bracelets and gold bangles. The dinner was being given outdoors by fire pit (with a roasted pig and dancing Zulu girls), so it was only fitting that Zorina be dressed summer-like and glamorous. At just seventeen years old, she was too stunning for words.

"The only thing I don't like", said Miss Lindy, "is the way the..."

Zorina already knew what it was. She had feared it, too.

"...well, your bottom fits the dress funny."

Zorina's heart sank, because it was her big butt that

was always messing up the shape of her clothes, and she was too skinny, way too thin to be cursed already with her mother's big fat firm, heartshaped ass. She burst into tears!

"Oh, Zorina...no, honey. Don't cry."

Zorina collapsed into Miss Lindy's arms. Her heart full with memories of the way her father had always teased her mother's backside by calling it "*funk-trunk*". It was such an ugly name, a cruel endearment. Etah had always hated it and yet Nopopie would go on and on about the *sweat* collecting between the crack...of Etah's funk-trunk.

"Now you listen to me...you look like a fashion model in that dress! Naomi Campbell would be proud! And as far as you being able to afford it...well, we'll just take a percentage from your salary every other week until it's paid for."

Zorina sobbered up immediately. She wanted to say: *Why don't we just pawn that award you're getting and pay for the dress--you selfish caucasoid bitch!* But, ofcourse, she didn't dare say it.

Thank God Cribbitch said it!

"Mummy!...Zorina's already earned that dress! She's the one who made all this beautiful glass that you're getting an award for. She shouldn't have to pay for that gown--rich as you and daddy are!"

Miss Lindy turned pink and relented.

But on the way back to the hotel, all Zorina could think about was the way that the black boys in her neighborhood were always dreaming of being rappers or athletes and how a girl like herself might be walking by and they might go: "Funk-trunk pussy stain...bang, bang, bang.....Funk-trunk pussy stain ...bang, bang, bang."

It was supposed to be a compliment. It was supposed to mean that she was sexually desirable. However, Zorina was smart enough to know the difference between a boy dreaming about banging up inside a hot-hole and a boy dreaming about *making love* to a girl. These boys, so dark and handsome, imagined her as nothing more than meat for sex.

Zorina figured that some unseen mystery girl, probably not from Sowego, was their choice for dreams about lovemaking, but whatever the case, she foolishly blamed her *funk-trunk* for her status with neighborhood boys.

The next night...Golf Theron arrived in Durban!

With his beautiful fiance', Maritza.

"I wouldn't miss your big night for the world, mother!"

Miss Lindy grinned, proudly, and kissed him and hugged him. "Oh, my baby boy!"

Zorina was dizzy with excitement--because Golf was going to get to see her all dressed up in her glamorous evening wear! It was just too good to be true!

But first...she was told to custom make Golf and Maritza's separate beds. So she went to their suite. First, she went into Golf's room and made his bed. Then she went to Maritza's room. There was music coming from the dressing room that led to the bathroom. It was Diana Ross singing, *"It's My House and I Live Here."* For some reason, hearing that song in Maritza's bathroom made Zorina intensely jealous. She didn't think that Diana Ross should be christening Maritza's territory.

She heard faint laughter.

Obviously, Golf was in the dressing room with Maritza. Zorina could smell him. His cologne. Then suddenly they laughed out really loud, Golf's voice proclaiming from behind the wall, "I must be in love with an angel!"

*I am an angel!...*Zorina wanted to proclaim out loud, as tears moistened her large brown eyes, not so much for Golf, but for the God who had cast her black and African.

Zorina couldn't help herself.

Really, she couldn't.

She went to the crack in the doorway of the dressing room and peeped inside.

Beautiful gowns, jewels...strewn everywhere.

Apparently, Maritza was trying on different outfits and Golf was there to lust over the creamy white contours of her incredibly tiny body. Her breasts, thought Zorina, were like slivers of liver hanging with big, cherry nipples. But her hair was incredible--flowing like gold all around her shoulders. Her face was so pale, like the Queen Elizabeth II portrait over Etah's bed. Pale like a queen.

"Is there anything I could want more than an angel?"

"Yes, a woman", replied Maritza.

Golf chuckled at her sharpness, and there was a way that he held her. Held her in his arms like she was grace itself. It was so incredibly endearing to Zorina's watching eyes. A kind of poetry in motion that she suddenly remembered dreaming about...wide awake sometimes, asleep other times. Now she remembered that she had dreamed about that kind of silly, emotional hanging on. Like in cinema films.

No. It was better than that. This couldn't be staged.

The way his eyes searched for Maritza in the mirror even though she was right up against him.

He loved her hair--he fingered around in it.

His chin rested on her shoulder and Zorina knew, intuitively, that they had never ever made love and that Maritza was a virgin. She just knew it.

"You smell like sunshine", he told Maritza.

"It's called *Privileage* by Dutchess Wayborn."

His hands fastened in front of her and his dreamy blue eyes closed and rocked her gently.

At the door, Zorina slid slowly, quietly, to the floor. There were no tears in her eyes now. She was totally engrossed in watching Golf behave just as she had dreamed he would.

"How many children should we have?"

"Two", she said. "A boy and a girl."

"Only two?", he growled.

Then he tickled her. She giggled and shook free of him.

Zorina noticed that they had the prettiest wine she had ever seen--sitting in glasses in front of the mirror. What beautiful color! What richness! It had to be absolutely delicious, Zorina thought, and her tastebuds suddenly went to fantasizing about what it must taste like. A wine that red and pretty. *I...made those glasses*, she suddenly realized.

Golf lifted a glass just then and took a swig from it. His white knuckles against the stem. Zorina's nipples hardened...her heart panted and her eyes felt as though someone had suddenly blown hard in them.

He put the rim of the glass to Maritza's thin rosy lips and she drank a swallow, comfortably closing her eyes and sinking back into the warmth of his chest.

"You make me so happy, Golf."

"I told you not to call me Golf when we're alone. Call me Noble."

She giggled and said, "Yes...*Noble*."

Zorina suddenly couldn't see a thing.

Not through her tears.

She went about the task of custom making Maritza's bed. Fluffing the pillows with an extra something--her admiration for Maritza. In and out of her mind, the memories of being raped by Golf Theron at thirteen sprung up like some annoying radio tune that she couldn't stop humming.

Tears fell off her chin...onto the lavish bedcovers.

Some old blues song was coming from the dressing room. A drunk lady singing out: *"...put that dog in the back-ah the house...tie 'em up; tie 'em up...hand me my pigfoot, hand me my beer!...tie 'em up; tie 'em up..."*

Zorina was done with the bed.

Just then...Golf came tumbling out of the dressing room. He halted as Zorina turned startled and said, "...Zorina!"

She wasn't accustomed to him calling her Zorina, so she said, "It's Zora to *you*...remember?"

Golf gulped. He came over to her and said in a low voice, "I really need to talk to you about something before you go to bed this evening. It's about us, Zorina. It's really important. Could you come to my room later--around midnight?"

About us Zorina.

That was so shocking to hear out of a white man's mouth and she couldn't believe that he was acknowledging that there was an *us* between them. Honestly, she had started to believe that she was just some fool traumatized by a rape, obsessed with getting from the rapist himself some kind of acceptance or forgiveness or approval.

But he had said *us* just now.

"Will you come, please?"

"Yes...Noble."

Miss Lindy was all teeth, wrinkles and huge blonde hair as she went up to receive the award for Glassmaker of the Year.

The entire dinner was for her. There were no competitors, no judges, no nominees. She thanked a long list of people, but not one of them was Zorina.

Othello came.

He had driven up with his wife LissaMondi, but some old white man had turned them away at the door and by the time Miss Lindy was told of it, it was too late.

Zorina could smell the smoke from the school again, but she tried not to let it get to her. She was the only black person at the whole affair and found herself roundly ignored.

Completely and absolutely.

For one thing--her young body in the strapless, tight white gown had upstaged all of the other women. The fact that she was such a pretty girl and the *only* oasis of colored skin in the room had made her into a striking kind of exotic goddess flower. It took Zorina a few hours to figure out that white people don't appreciate it when a black woman does something that only white women are supposed to be able to do. They could accept her as a young, raggedy maid--but not as a beautiful black woman *of childbearing age.*

The biggest surprise was Golf's strange behavior.

He didn't look at Zorina one...single...time. Even when she spoke to him (to get him to look) he acted as if she were butt naked or something. The other men seemed to sweat whenever she walked by them. They clung to their wives and girlfriends as if they felt literally threatened. Zorina felt dirty, because not even the waiters and maids (all Indians and Asians) would acknowledge her presence or her beauty. Cribbitch was too young to attend the party and Maritza Buitengracht simply didn't socialize with kaffir girls in public, period.

Out of great fires, the breathtaking glasses that Zorina had created lined their velvet tiers like trophies, and increasingly, Zorina wanted to scream out that *she* was the one who had formed and sculpted everyone of them by hand! It was *her* they gathered to honor--the kaffir girl! All of this glassed beauty was because of the monumental sorrow that had pushed forth her genius, but she couldn't do that to the Theron family and get away with it. The cost would be too high. Like the mice who lived in the walls back home, the white people scampered around merrily, careful not to make eye contact or place themselves in the open, away from the safety of the walls. How many souls had they nibbled on to stand here munching caviar and sipping martinis--and why did Zorina want so desperately to be acknowledged and accepted by them?

By the end of the night, Zorina felt as if she were just a coffee stain on somebody's white silk lap napkin.

She made it to Golf and Maritza's suite at two in the morning. Golf , who seemed to have been waiting by the door, let her in and then quickly rushed her through the black darkness to the lighted doorway of his room. It had been years since his hands had gripped Zorina's body this way and she thought she might pee on herself from the adrenaline that was pulsing through her veins as his large white hands tightened around her soft little cinnamon-stick arm.

"Don't make a sound", he whispered harshly, his breath smelling like liverwurst and scotch, and there was no more music, no more light coming from Maritza's room. Just black silence--her door closed.

Slowly, Golf closed the door to his own room and Zorina wondered how she should act? She had seen Halle Berry in a cinema film and liked the combination of vulnerability and strength that the actress possessed. She thought she could act like that and stand her ground no matter what he said. She might even get loud if he said the wrong thing...so that people would wonder what a little kaffir girl had been doing in the privacy of his room at such an ungodly hour.

But just then, Golf flicked off the lights.

The room went black and she felt him grab her. His hands digging in to the plushness of her ass and his wet, dirty mouth kissing and biting against her neck and shoulders!

He panted: "Don't fight it, Zora."

One of his white fingers was plunging between the crack of her ass. Her panties, she felt, were being dragged off.

Her eyes bulged, swelling with tears, and she couldn't speak or make a sound--she was so shocked to be getting what she had thought she wanted. Not sex. But just *man-woman attention* from a man that she was infatuated by and supposedly wasn't good enough to have.

But she hadn't expected it to feel this disrespectul, this dirty, and yet intellectually, *and by memory*...she had known that it would.

Her mind told her to scream. To make him stop.

Men like Golf had kicked holes in her father's stomach and taken credit for the art that African people created. Men like Golf had called black mothers *apes* and taught little black boys to do the same. Men like Golf had raped little black girls and fully expected those little girls to behave as friends the very next day. Men like Golf knew about selfish greed. They knew all about people that were weaker than them.

You don't deserve this!, some voice inside Zorina seemed to be raging. But Noble was tearing her breasts loose now. Young and high they jiggled in his hands and got caught in his slobbering mouth! Zorina's dress stank already, she realized, and it was smudged and soiled and torn, and so she merely braced the cold air as it came off. Her soft, hot flesh instantly being dug into by what seemed like the hands of many. He hurt her privates by wetting his fingers in her lips.

He didn't guide her to the bed--he bent her naked ass down to the floor.

Zorina wanted to stop him, but she didn't have the courage to stop him. She could feel her mother's slap against her face and she didn't know if she was good enough to demand to be treated with affection and tenderness.

"Oh, you sweet dirty little bitch", he moaned in ecstacy as he licked her neck, slobbered her mouth and bit at her nipples like a dog pup fighting to get milk.

There was no mention of her smelling like sunshine.

His thick white dick (penis, prick) went up in her.

The pain of it shooting through her body and ripping the tight skin of her pink opening. She was already bleeding.

His hand stifled the scream and her tears poured down the sides of her face, but she kept her weeping *restrained* so that no one would come and see what Golf really thought of her or find out how worthless a stain she really was.

She closed her eyes and tried to leave her body. She tried, desperately, to pretend that it was the kingish and very beautiful actor Djimon Hounsou inside her. Her favorite cinema idol. Then she could like it and want it.

But her mind wasn't strong enough to create all that.

It was Golf Theron banging her dirty little coffee stain!

Worthless kaffir trash bitch! That's what she called herself. Dirty, nasty little worthless piece of nothing.

nigger bitch.

Golf suddenly put his elbow in her mouth to brace the sound. Then he dramatically increased the swagger and the anxiousness of his beastfucking.

The pain shot through Zorina's body and she could hear the rythm of the black boys as they chanted, rooting Golf on, cheering: "Funk-trunk pussy stain...bang, bang, bang." You have to get the flow of a rapper and picture a cute South African girl with a plump, tight ass and say it faster: "Funk-trunk pussy stain...bang, bang, bang!"

Funk-trunk pussy stain...bang, bang, bang!

Golf jumped up off her!

His dick was all bloody and he was coming.

He shoved his penis into Zorina's wet face and shot off his wad with a fierce stifled groan.

His chest heaved with heavy breathing and his wet, hot sticky jism ran in her eyes and all down the sides of her face.

"Wash yourself off, Zora...I got to git me rest, eh."

Golf was exhausted.

As Zorina lay on the floor, she could not seem to pull herself from the fire this time. Her classmates' screaming seemed to form a kind of chorus to a lullaby. The cinders were hot, but cold, too...this time. Eve smiled at her and handed her the knife. Eve kissed her on the cheek.

The knife?

Zorina didn't remember there being a knife in her hand, but suddenly, there was...and she was floating through the hotel's corridors. As if suspended just above the plush carpet.

In one hand she held the knife...and in the other...Golf Theron's white dick and his pink hairy sack; all bloody.

That seemed awfully odd.

Ugly, too. The sound of Maritza's high pitched screams.

Zorina ran out of the hotel.

The police hadn't put the bullet between her eyes yet.

So she ran...freer than she'd ever been. Down to the street til she reached the docks. She stood there...staring out at the shiny black sea.

Beautiful ocean...becoming more and more of itself.

She didn't hear the sirens of the police automobiles.

No. She heard the drunk blues woman singing from America: "...*that front porch...that's one dayyyn-jerus PLACE.*"

They called Zorina's name. So she turned around.

The gunshots sounded so far away; annoying.

So she turned back around.

She saw two people...walking on water! Walking right across the sea, swiftly coming towards her.

It was Jesus Christ with charcoal black Eve!

Coming to get her, she realized.

Jesus didn't look anything like the effeminate Christ that the whites always portrayed. He was tall and buff, dark like a Mexican or some other sexy latin breed of king...he had wet curly black hair and suave, sensuous bedroom eyes.

He reached out his hand to Zorina and said, "Don't be affraid of the way it feels..."

To her stunned surprise, she had already fallen into the water. But now Jesus Christ lifted her to her feet. She stood, quite astonished, atop the water's surface.

She and Eve embraced as tightly as long lost sisters!

"I hope you won't miss the fire", said Eve.

"I won't", said Zorina.

"We have a new life for you", said Nopopie, Zorina's father, as he stepped out of the fog...and into the moonlight. Zorina ran into his arms. She was so overjoyed! "Oh, daddy", she cried. "Without a father, life is so hard!"

Then Jesus Christ, whose wet honey-bronzed chest stuck out like a shield of faith, asked her, "Do you have any last words before we leave this place?"

Zorina's eyes filled with tears, because for a moment, she felt human again. She thought of how some whites had often called black women *mules*. A mule is a small brown donkey that stinks and is considered ugly and used exclusively for servitude. A mule's stinking baby is called a mulatto.

"Yes...I do."

She turned and looked at the lights of the now crowded pier, legions of superior white faces around the ambulances, the fire brigades, South Africa's evil police.

From an *irrevocable* soul, Zora promised Jesus Christ: "The black woman...is the meteor...that is coming to this earth!"

Interview
with
KOLA BOOF

*Interview with Kola Boof
   reprinted by permission of
   the Amsterdam African News
   Authority.

**Kola Boof (pregnant with a bowl over her stomach) appears on the back
cover of this book. Photo by Kangman.

Omar Aberjan's infamous interview with Kola Boof (Amsterdam African News Authority--November 23, 1999). Reprinted here in its entirety.

Omar Aberjan:

"Hello, Kola."

KOLA BOOF:

"Hi, Omar."

Omar Aberjan:

"Let me first preface our meeting by mentioning how much you hate being interviewed--you say it's your least favorite thing in the whole world, but for the sake of clearing up some very nasty rumors about your late father--you've agreed to speak with us. I'm very pleased. I guess we'll start with your father and then we'll talk about your work as a writer."

KOLA BOOF:

"That's fine."

Omar Aberjan:

"Your father **(Egyptian entrapeneur and archeologist Harith Bin Farouk)** was killed when..."

161

KOLA BOOF: (interrupts)

"Not killed, Ahmad. Murdered."

Omar Aberjan:

"..yes, sorry. He was murdered when you were just a kid, because he spoke out against Sudan's Islamic government and specifically against slavery in The Sudan. And now that you've been launched as an actress, and much more importantly, a writer--there are rumors coming out of Sudan that your father was himself a slave trader. People who knew your family are saying that he wasn't even Sudanese and that he was a heroin addict. They're saying he beat your mother."

KOLA BOOF:

"My father died...because he tried to stop slavery from taking place in Sudan. He was a member of the Sudanese People's Liberation Army. Only the lowest sandnigger would make up such evil lies about him. He was from Egypt, but he lived in Sudan almost his entire adult life, and because he was Sunni Muslim and extremely lightskinned, he was not viewed as African--but that's what my Mahdi Pappuh considered himself, African. He felt that he was a black man and he married my mother because he wanted BLACK children. He stated that many, many times. He never EVER beat my mother, he treated her like a queen! He was an exceptional husband and the perfect father!"

Omar Aberjan:

"But wasn't he a heroin addict, Kola?"

KOLA BOOF:

"Yes...he was a heroin addict. So what."

Omar Aberjan:

"And you're categorically denying all the reports that he himself kidnapped Sudanese people and sold them as slaves?"

KOLA BOOF:

"My father would have BEEN a slave before he sold one--I stake my life on that. He was in no way involved in anything but the struggle to secure freedom and equal rights for black people in Sudan. The people who are making these lies are the same people, the murhaleen, that had him murdered--they want to shut me up, because they know I'll advance my father's causes, and because I'm a woman and I'm saying whatever the hell I please. They want to use my father to hurt my credibility--but my father was a hero. I take great pride in being his daughter."

Omar Aberjan:

"Do you ever fear for your own safety?"

KOLA BOOF: (long pause)

"I'm an orphan, Ahmad. I'm too vulnerable to be affraid of ANYONE. Anybody who wants to kick my ass...may as well just get in line. This is my only life and I'm going to do with it what I want. No one's going to stop me. I say this to the little children--'they can only kill you ONCE, so start some shit'."

(continued...)

Omar Aberjan:

"As we move along to discuss your work as a writer--what do you say to some Arab people who feel that you're prejudiced against Arabs and that you constantly paint an unflattering portrait of Arabs in your work?"

KOLA BOOF:

"The people who made me an orphan and ran me out of my country were Arabs. The people who are raping Sudan and making it a slave state are Arabs. The people of Egypt, which is a nation that I am deeply ashamed to be related to, they are Arabs. So I don't give a shit what Arab people think about me. The fact has always been, no matter what they tell you in America--that Arab people are a great historical enemy to African people. So no, I don't like Arabs. I feel triumphant saying it in public."

Omar Aberjan:

"Well, I am Arabic AND African and I have to disagree with your position, but we'll move on."

KOLA BOOF:

"Don't ask me something if you don't want the answer. That's why I don't do interviews. Interviews make me look hard and unkind, because I don't have patience and I'm very passionate about whatever it is I believe. It's better not to do interviews."

Omar Aberjan: (clears throat)

"A lot of people feel that by appearing topless on the back

of your book covers, you're exploiting a kind of backwards romanticism about African women and you're trying to draw attention to yourself without letting your talent do the talking..."

KOLA BOOF: (interrupts)
"The reason I am topless on the back of my book jackets--and always will be--is because one hundred years from now, I want people to realize that African women who walked around naked all day were also capable of writing books and having complex opinions and creating perspective out of sorrow. That's been a fact for thousands of years, but this is my way, personally, of demonstrating that fact. I also choose to be topless, because it is not Christian; it is not Islamic. I am not ashamed when I see the women of my land walking around naked with baskets on their heads. That's MY statement to the world."

Omar Aberjan:
"Are you angry?"

KOLA BOOF:
"Do I sound angry?"

Omar Aberjan:
"Actually, you don't. You're very soft-spoken and extremely feminine. You behave more like a sex kitten than an activist or a writer, but in the content of your conversation and the kind of stories that you write--there's this dazzling anger."
continued...

KOLA BOOF:

"Well, as long as it's dazzling, darling." **(laughs)**

Omar Aberjan:

"So are you angry?"

KOLA BOOF:

"Well, let me put it this way--I don't care if people think I am. But I don't know what to say. How does one explain one's self when so much of the work that one does is based on so much raw reality and desperation? My work mostly makes me intensely horny, because I want the burn to go away. But I feel that I have to write what I write. I get nose bleeds writing, because I get so passionate about it. I cry out loud in places. It's the reason I'm not good for doing interviews. I don't know how to make people like me--but I do know how to tell them what I think, and giving interviews is all about manipulating people in to liking you. I'm not sure that I WANT to be liked."

Omar Aberjan: (laughs)

"Something makes me like you, Kola. You're different."

KOLA BOOF: (laughs)

"Thank you, Ahmad. I'm nervous more than anything."

Omar Aberjan:

"So when did you know that you wanted to be a writer?"

(continued)

KOLA BOOF:

"Well, before I could want to write, I had to really love to READ--the first book that I ever read isn't considered great literature, but it was a book that really got me addicted to reading and that was Jaqueline Susann's "Valley of the Dolls". I was fourteen and I was just starting to really speak English good. I learned English mainly by watching a soap opera, Another World. But anyway, I loved that novel, so I looked for another book to read...and that's when I found this novel featuring a little black girl who looked Sudani to me. It was the second book I read. THE BLUEST EYE by Toni Morrison...oh, yes."

Omar Aberjan:

"Wow. You look like it meant a lot to you."

KOLA BOOF:

"As an African child suddenly living in America, I can't tell you what that book meant to me, because...well...it's like living in a strange paradise for several years, quietly aware of the dirty little secret that Black Americans guard and deny...and so when I read BLUEST EYE, I felt that for the first time since I'd set foot in America--someone was finally telling me the truth. Straight up, just the way I had witnessed it and felt it. To come from Sudan is to feel the colorism, the shame, the class distinctions-- super intensified. In America, you constantly realize that your skin is black--but in Africa, ALL decent human beings are black. Just as natural as being white. So reading BLUEST EYE was like reading *l*etters from a person in hell--if there's any

God in you, you just have to write back. I felt so blessed."

Omar Aberjan:

"And so you decided to become a writer?"

KOLA BOOF:

"*Not* at fifteen, no. But I did think that Toni Morrison was the smartest, most truthful, most beautiful woman that I had ever seen--and at fifteen, she was the third woman that I wanted to be. The first one was Gladys Knight and the second one was Diana Ross. I always had idols and heroines that I admired, and subsequently, I would pattern myself after those images. Carol Burnett, Bette Davis, Nawal El Sadaawi, Grace Jones, Maxine Waters, Anna Magnani, Sigourney Weaver, Barbara Bush."

Omar Aberjan: (laughing)

"*You're hilarious!*"

KOLA BOOF:

"I'm dead serious. It felt like America was killing my soul and I needed these images to help me invent myself as a woman. In retrospect and in particular, I think that women like Toni Morrison and Alice Walker and Oprah have been mothers to many young black girls who didn't know what to think about life or themselves. Oh, I'm glad I mentioned Alice Walker, because I really, really love her. She is so incredibly RIGHT. And she and Toni Morrison--and as a writer, I don't think I'll ever be in their league--but women like Alice Walker and Toni Morrison are

168

more than just writers and artists...now listen...just as much as Malcolm X and Dr. King and Marcus Garvey...Alice Walker and Toni Morrison were important revolutionaries. They have affected the lifestyles and social changes in American people just as dramatically as any civil rights leader has. If not more. But because it's the female energy they cultivated, well. And what I cherish most about those two women is that they remained AUTHENTIC black women. They preserved the best ways of their mothers and grandmothers and they always reached for the blackest part of the heart, the sweetest part. They recognized me as a human being by recognizing themselves. Unconditionally. They remind me of the Zarpunni wisdom women back in Sudan. I love reading Gloria Naylor, Audre Lord, Maya Angelou, Pearl Cleage, Zora Neal Hurston and that new lady, Bebe Moore Campbell is good. Gwendolyn Brooks. But these women are social activists and they breastfeed their nation. That's what we women are for. To breastfeed, be spiritbound and have sexual power within the society. It takes a womb to make a man. "

Omar Aberjan:

"I don't really know enough about American life to comment."

KOLA BOOF:

"America is the greatest country on earth. I mean, there really is NO GOOD place to live on earth--but atleast in America you can be yourself and be a damned fool to your heart's content. I went from total sadness to total triumph in America, because they allow a woman to blossom here--if she's not too obsessed with being a victim. I think Capitalism is great. I like it, because I could become a one woman conglomerate here. It's like living on top of a lavishly beautiful and stale snow white wedding cake. The rest of the world is just mush, sad to say."

Omar Aberjan:
"Are you going to appear in any more films?"

KOLA BOOF: (Silenced because they had agreed not to mention her daring sex symbol cameos in Egyptian cinema.)

Omar Aberjan: (Grinning from ear to ear)
"I'm sorry, Kola. We won't open that can."

KOLA BOOF:
"Anybody who knows me knows that I really love films, I'm a silent movie buff, mainly. I'll always hunger for films, but I won't ever appear in one again unless I can control the story and the way that my character is presented. I'd like to play Alice Walker or Sojourner Truth or a really clever whore who prostitutes herself to start her own church. I think I might like to become a director one day to have creative control. I love films more than any other art form to be honest, but the dark nympho I've been in Egypt--I wouldn't mind if those films just disappeared from the face of the earth. In fact, if I have anything to do with it, they will."

Continued...

170

Omar Aberjan:

"What do you look for in a man, Kola?"

KOLA BOOF:

"I can make do with just about any kind of man, I think. I don't know what I look for--a man has to show me what I want. Every man is different. But I like extremely dark men who love reggae music and like to play chess and drive red cars and drink beer on weekends and have incredibly muscular bodies and like to spoil women. I love men despite what some people think. And I need them for sex."

Omar Aberjan:

"One of the characters in your stories said that she wouldn't mind being a lesbian, because she thinks it's easier. Is that how you feel, too?"

KOLA BOOF:

"Well, I'm not lesbian or bisexual, and I never will be, but I do envy lesbians, because they don't seem used up by what men do. They aren't obsessed with men like the rest of us are. They're free to just not give a shit about men and I wish I could be that way. Plus, I think women are kinder, more loyal than men are. A lot of my personal heroes happen to be lesbians."

Continued

Omar Aberjan:

"You pretty much denounce Islam in your work and you're definitely no christian, so what are your religious beliefs?"

KOLA BOOF:

"I believe that love is for everyone, period. And I believe that the purpose of life is that your deeds outlive you. But I don't like to talk about religion. I believe in one God. I respect my ancestors. I know that I am responsible for all mankind, even the people I don't like. God requires that we love one another. That's all I'll say."

Omar Aberjan:

"Our ancient ancestors whorshipped the Sun and other pagan Gods. Do you try to preserve the old ways?"

KOLA BOOF:

"I do what Kola's heart and mind leads Kola to do, period. I don't want to discuss this, Omar."

Omar Aberjan:

"O.K., on a lighter note--are your breasts real?"
(laughs) Just kidding. God is great!"

KOLA BOOF: (not laughing)

"Yes, my breasts are real, Omar. They're all natural. You want me to let them sit out while you interview me?"
continued

172

Omar Aberjan:

"That would be too wonderful, Kola, because I never got over that dance scene in _____. I have to tell you, wow!"

KOLA BOOF:

"You don't really think I'm going to sit here topless do you? God! I wish people would understand that a woman's bare breasts are a religious symbol, just like a crucifix is! You being from an African mother, you should know that Omar. The notion that breasts are a sex object is a western phenomenon. I can't believe you see my image as sexual."

Omar Aberjan:

"Well, maybe you're in denial Kola, because I think your literature and the dance scene in _____ is purely sexual. I see you as a very sexual creature. I don't think you're a religious symbol at all. Not your bare breasts anyway. When I look at you, I think of relaxing on the Nile and having hot pagan sex with a very exotic woman."

KOLA BOOF: (eyes downcast, mad)

"Next question, Omar."

"Kaaahhh....Let's get this interview over with."

Omar Aberjan:

"Kola, I'm just repeating what a lot of men who've read your book think."

continued

KOLA BOOF:

"Well, you know what? No matter what anybody thinks, I take my work very seriously. I consider myself an artist and I think that what I have to say is tangible and important. I don't care how men see me, Omar. If they think I'm a sex object, that's on them. I see my image as sensuous more than sexual. I am like a woman breastfeeding. I think my flesh is soft and beautiful, but inside me, there's a great fire. I want to say things from my own perspective. I've listened to the rest of the world all my life, and you know what? The world *lies* on black women. And it tries to make the African black woman invisible alltogether. I rebel against that! I have something to say and it's not necessarily what people are used to, but I believe my life has purpose in this way. So my bare breasts are presented as a spiritual gift. That is my intention and that is my mark against the eyesight of all the trangressors of my people. I want them to see my black breasts exposed and know that I am from someplace else and that my passion and wisdom doesn't come merely from association with them. I want to stand for my own ancestral mothers--who were always bare in the sun and gave birth to this whole world."

Omar Aberjan:

"I understand, Kola. Now...what about the female characters in your short stories? How much of that is actually you?"

KOLA BOOF:

"None of my characters are me. Not if you pay attention."

Omar Aberjan:

"Kola, I can see you're very mad at me at this point, and I apologize if I've...you're becoming this underground star..."

KOLA BOOF: (Smiles and interrupts)

"I'm not mad at all Mr. Aberjan. Listen...your job is to interview people, if it were my job, I'd be even tougher and dicier than you are. But I don't want this opportunity to go by without some real sense of my purpose as an artist being acknowledged...that's all, dollface. Every since "The Goddess Flower" came out, people seem to want stardom and fame for me, because they think I'm provocative, they see dollar signs in the way that I approach art. Stardom, fame and being provocative are honestly not what I'm seeking, Omar. I am seeking voices that can record the faces around me from my own perspective. I am blessed to be African and also to be empowered by American methods of self-assertiveness, so I see myself as an experimental artist...I'm an underground star, but it's not stardom that means anything at all if there is no tangible message."

Omar Aberjan:

"Where do you see yourself in ten years, Kola?"

KOLA BOOF:

"Well, first let me finish what I was saying, because I see like this...the Black Americans are the only Black people on earth to have access to the media. That is my someday hoped for core audience--especially as an African artist. I feel that we must begin to make an impact on their way of thinking and behaving both parentally and emotionally--as Africans, no matter what they've been told--we have that right. For instance, I don't see why we continue to line up to see this painting, THE MONA LISA, and regard it as great, great art...but fail to notice that today's equivalent to the MONA LISA is the cover photo of a music album...Grace Jones's ISLAND LIFE...now that's great, great art! And where is the naked form of all womankind better represented than there? But, ofcourse, people would laugh at me."

Omar Aberjan:

"I don't know if I've ever seen that album cover."

KOLA BOOF:

"Well it's not just an album cover--it's one of the greatest artistic masterpieces of modern times, equal to anything they rave and holler about Andy Warhol for, but that's what I'm saying. I don't like in America when the negroes spend all their time trying to befriend and be caretaker of other races and then fail to preserve the beauty and the uniqueness of their own authentic identity. It sickens me, because the race of Black humans is a race and it deserves better than that. It shouldn't be compromised with all this sentimental assimilation and mixed-race face masks creating that shadow...it should be unleashed freely as just what it is, in its natural form. Otherwise it is still enslaved, it is still a servant to the whims of alien outsiders. That is my message to Black Americans and that is my art's genesis. I am peeling away the religions imposed, the sexual object...excuse me...sexual object-

-ifications imposed and the (Euro-centrism) that is more than just imposed, but imbeded...I cannot love Black American people and give them any other message than the most African one I can provide. That is my contribution, whether it is right, wrong, appreciated or not appreciated...I will someday die knowing that I did what my ancestors asked of me. I trust my judgement, Omar. There are lots of new black women artists in America that I admire--Charlayne Woodard, Kasi Lemons, Vivica A. Fox, Cheryl Dunye, Lauryn Hill, Queen Latifah, Sudan's own Alek Wek--and they are urging black women in America to reinvent themselves--which is long overdue. They are different than me, but I, too, am part of that generation, except my message is more coarse. It's the only message I have, goddamnit, but I bring it with love. That's what Kola Boof and her naked breasts and her art is about. Bringing something to the pot and saying what I have to say to the Black Americans."

Omar Aberjan:

"It's really ironic that your work is available everywhere BUT in Black America--has "Goddess Flower" been published in America yet? I don't think black americans have even heard of you, have they?"

KOLA BOOF:

"No, but I live in America, and trust me, I will conquer America. It will just take time. Even in Europe, I am so underground that people can't locate my work. You would be surprised at how hard it is to establish contact. One problem is that white women don't like my work, they don't think I paint them in a flattering light. And I refuse to. So that cuts out a big patron of the arts and major publishing realm right there."

Omar Aberjan:

"That reminds me of a line in one of your short stories that really offended me...and that was the one when the woman said, and I quote..."The black man is the biggest disappointment since God". That just blew me away, Kola. I kept asking myself--how could Kola write that? How could she?"

KOLA BOOF:

"Well, shit. How could I NOT?"

Omar Aberjan:

"So you really feel that way yourself, Kola? I thought you loved black men."

KOLA BOOF:

"I do love black men, but that's irrelevent. The most important thing, and I would like to end our interview with this sentence, Omar--but the most important thing is that the black woman is the meteor that is coming to this earth. Say it with me..."

Omar and KOLA: (together, laughing)

"The black woman is the meteor that is coming to this earth!"

Omar Aberjan:

"You know, that reminds me, Kola--I really didn't like that last story, "DAY OF VOW". That was so...disturbing. The way the characters that killed people went to heaven and all. I thought it was over the top."

KOLA BOOF:

"'DAY OF VOW'" is probably the most misunderstood story that I ever wrote. I know it's wild, it's out there, but what it's really about is the need for revolution in one's life. Especially in the lives of black women, they get so used to a station...I know all these women who are waiting on Jesus to change their destiny or they mistakenly believe that the more they suffer, the more they'll be blessed during after-life. I think that's cowardly and it's a cop-out. I believe in changing ones own life...changing your destiny, your situation. I believe in revolution and I wish that women would learn to fight half as hard for themselves as they fight for the men they love. It's always the man's revolution we uphold--but what about our own needs? That's what that story is about, Omar. It's about the need to be willfull when all that's left is being a victim. A smart woman embraces revolution."

Omar Aberjan:

"O.K., since you're so charming...we'll end it like this, Kola. The black woman...is the meteor ...that is coming to this earth."